"You don't like ~~~~~~, much, do you, Daisy?"

"I don't know anything about you, Dr. Seymour."

"An indisputable fact. You haven't answered my question."

"Yes, I have—I don't know you well enough to know, do I?"

"No? Personally, I know if I like or dislike someone the moment I set eyes on them."

"Well, we're all different, aren't we?" she said primly. The mocking look he gave her sent the color into her cheeks.

Betty Neels spent her childhood and youth in Devonshire before training as a nurse and midwife. She was an army nursing sister during the war, married a Dutchman and subsequently lived in Holland for fourteen years. She lives with her husband in Dorset, and has a daughter and grandson. Her hobbies are reading, animals—she owns a matronly cat— old buildings and writing. Betty began to write after her retirement from nursing, incited by a lady in a library bemoaning the lack of romance novels.

Books by Betty Neels

A VALENTINE
FOR DAISY
Betty Neels

Harlequin Books

TORONTO • NEW YORK • LONDON
AMSTERDAM • PARIS • SYDNEY • HAMBURG
STOCKHOLM • ATHENS • TOKYO • MILAN
MADRID • WARSAW • BUDAPEST • AUCKLAND

ISBN 0-373-03347-8

A VALENTINE FOR DAISY

Copyright © 1993 by Betty Neels.

First North American Publication 1995.

CHAPTER ONE

THE hazy sunshine of a late July afternoon highlighted the steady stream of small children issuing from one of the solid Victorian houses in the quiet road. It was an orderly exit; Mrs Gower-Jones, who owned the nursery school and prided herself upon its genteel reputation, frowned upon noisy children. As their mothers and nannies, driving smart little Fiats, larger Mercedes and Rovers, arrived, the children gathered in the hall, and were released under the eye of whoever was seeing them off the premises.

Today this was a small, rather plump girl whose pale brown hair was pinned back into a plaited knot, a style which did nothing for her looks: too wide a mouth, a small pert nose and a determined chin, the whole redeemed from plainness by a pair of grey eyes fringed with curling mousy lashes. As Mrs Gower-Jones so often complained to the senior of her assistants, the girl had no style although there was no gainsaying the fact that the children liked her; moreover even the most tiresome child could be coaxed by her to obedience.

The last child seen safely into maternal care, the girl closed the door and crossed the wide hall to the first of the rooms on either side of it. There were two girls there, clearing away the results of the children's activities. They were too young for lessons but they spent their day modelling clay, painting, playing simple games and being read to, and the mess at the end of the afternoon was considerable.

They both looked up as the girl joined them. 'Thank heaven for Saturday tomorrow!' exclaimed the older of the girls. 'Pay day too. Ron's driving me to Dover this evening; we're going over to Boulogne to do some shopping.' She swept an armful of coloured bricks into a plastic bucket. 'What about you, Mandy?'

The other girl was wiping a small table clean. 'I'm going down to Bournemouth—six of us—it'll be a bit of a squeeze in the car but who cares? There's dancing at the Winter Gardens.'

They both looked at the girl who had just joined them. 'What about you, Daisy?'

They asked her every Friday, she thought, not really wanting to know, but not wanting to be unfriendly. She said now, as she almost always did, 'Oh, I don't know,' and smiled at them, aware that though they liked her they thought her rather dull and pitied her for the lack of excitement in her life. Well, it wasn't exciting but, as she told herself shortly from time to time, she was perfectly content with it.

It took an hour or more to restore the several play-rooms to the state of perfection required by Mrs Gower-Jones; only then, after she had inspected them, did she hand over their pay packets, reminding them, quite unnecessarily, to be at their posts by half-past eight on Monday morning.

Mandy and the older girl, Joyce, hurried away to catch the minibus which would take them to Old Sarum where they both lived, and Daisy went round the back of the house to the shed where she parked her bike. It was three miles to Wilton from Salisbury and main road all the way; she didn't much like the journey, though, for the traffic was always heavy, especially at this time of the year with the tourist season not yet over even though the schools had returned. She cycled down the quiet road and presently circled the roundabout and joined the stream of homegoing traffic, thinking of the weekend ahead of her. She went over the various duties awaiting her without self-pity; she had shouldered them cheerfully several years earlier when her father had died and her mother, cosseted all her married life, had been completely lost, unable to cope with the bills, income tax and household expenses with which he had always dealt. Daisy had watched her mother become more and more depressed and muddled and finally she had taken over, dealing tidily with the household finances and shielding her mother from business worries.

In this she had been considerably helped by her young sister. Pamela was still at school, fifteen years old, clever and bent on making a name for herself but understanding that her mother had led a sheltered life which made it impossible for her to stand on her own two feet. She knew that it was hard luck on Daisy, although they never discussed it, but she had the good sense to see that there was nothing much to be done about it. Daisy was a darling but she had never had a boyfriend and it had to be faced—she had no looks to speak of. Pamela, determined to get as many A levels as possible, go to college and take up the scientific career she had decided upon, none the less intended to marry someone rich who would solve all their problems. She had no doubts about this since she was a very pretty girl and knew exactly what she wanted from life.

Daisy wove her careful way through the fast-flowing traffic, past the emerging tourists from Wilton House, and turned left at the centre of the crossroads in the middle of the little town. Her father had worked in the offices of the Wilton estate and she had been born and lived all her life in the small cottage, the end one of a row backing the high walls surrounding the park, on the edge of the town. She wheeled her bike through the gate beside the house, parked it in the shed in the back garden and went indoors.

Her mother was in the kitchen, sitting at the table, stringing beans. She was small like Daisy, her hair still only faintly streaked with grey, her pretty face marred by a worried frown.

'Darling, it's lamb chops for supper but I forgot to buy them...'

Daisy dropped a kiss on her parent's cheek. 'I'll go for them now, Mother, while you make the tea. Pam will lay the table when she gets in.'

She went back to the shed and got out her bike and cycled back to the crossroads again. The butcher was halfway down the row of shops on the other side but as she reached the traffic-lights they turned red and she put a foot down, impatient to get across. The traffic was heavy now and the light was tantalisingly slow. A car drew up beside her and she turned to look at it. A dark grey Rolls-Royce. She eyed it appreciatively, starting at the back and allowing her eyes to roam to its bonnet until she became aware of the driver watching her.

She stared back, feeling for some reason foolish, frowning a little at the thin smile on his handsome face. He appeared to be a big man, his hair as dark as his heavy-lidded eyes . . . it was a pity that the lights changed then and the big car had slid silently away before she was back in the saddle, leaving her with the feeling that something important to her had just happened. 'Ridiculous,' she said so loudly that a passer-by on the pavement looked at her oddly.

Pamela was home when she got back and together they set about preparing their supper before sitting down in the pleasant little sitting-room to drink the tea Mrs Pelham had made.

'Been a nice day; have you enjoyed it?' asked Pamela, gobbling biscuits.

'It's not been too bad. The new children seem all right. I've got four this term—that makes fifteen. Two of the new ones are twins, a girl and a boy, and I suspect that they're going to be difficult . . .'

'I thought Mrs Gower-Jones only took children from suitable families.' Mrs Pelham smiled across at her daughter.

'Oh, they're suitable—their father's a baronet or something,' said Daisy vaguely. 'They're almost four years old and I think they'll drive me mad by the end of the term.'

Pamela laughed. 'And it's only just begun . . .'

They talked about something else then and after supper Daisy sat down at the table, doling out the housekeeping money, school bus fares, pocket money, and then she put what was over—and there wasn't much—into the old biscuit tin on the kitchen mantelpiece. They managed—just—on her wages and her mother's pension; just for a while after her father's death they had got into difficulties and her mother had appealed to her for help, and ever since then Daisy sat down every Friday evening, making a point of asking her mother's advice about the spending of their income. Mrs Pelham always told her to do whatever was best, but all the same Daisy always asked. She loved her mother dearly, realising that she had had a sheltered girlhood and marriage and needed to be taken care of—something which she and Pamela did to the best of their ability, although Daisy was aware that within a few years Pamela would leave home for a university and almost certainly she would marry. About her own future Daisy didn't allow herself to bother overmuch. She had friends, of course, but none of the young men she knew had evinced the slightest desire to fall in love with her and, studying her ordinary face in her dressing-table mirror, she wasn't surprised. It was a pity she had no chance to train for something; her job was pleasant enough, not well paid but near her home and there were holidays when she could catch up on household chores and see to the garden.

She was a sensible girl, not given to discontent, although she dreamed of meeting a man who would fall in love with her, marry her and take over the small burdens of her life. He would need to have money, of course, and a pleasant house with a large garden where the children would be able to play. It was a dream she didn't allow herself to dwell upon too often.

The weekend went far too quickly as it always did. She took her mother shopping and stopped for coffee in the little town while Pam stayed at home studying, and after lunch Daisy went into the quite big garden and grubbed up weeds, hindered by Razor the family cat, a dignified middle-aged beast who was as devoted to them all as they were to him. On Sunday they went to church and, since it was a sultry day, spent the rest of the day in the garden.

Daisy left home first on Monday morning; Mrs Gower-Jones liked her assistants to be ready and waiting when the first of the children arrived at half-past eight, which meant that Daisy had to leave home an hour earlier than that. The sultriness had given way to thundery rain and the roads were wet and slippery. She was rounding the corner by Wilton House when she skidded and a car braked to a sudden halt inches from her back wheel.

She put a foot to the ground to balance herself and looked over her shoulder. It was the Rolls-Royce, and the same man was driving it; in other circumstances she would have been delighted to see him again, for she had thought of him several times during the weekend, but now her feelings towards him were anything but friendly.

'You are driving much too fast,' she told him severely. 'You might have killed me.'

'Thirty miles an hour,' he told her unsmilingly, 'and you appear alive to me.' His rather cool gaze flickered over her plastic mac with its unbecoming hood framing her ordinary features. She chose to ignore it.

'Well, drive more carefully in future,' she advised him in the voice she used to quell the more recalcitrant of the children at Mrs Gower-Jones's.

She didn't wait for his answer but got on her bike and set off once more, and when the big car slid gently past

her she didn't look at its driver, although she was sorely
tempted to do so.

She was the first to arrive and Mrs Gower-Jones was
already there, poking her rather sharp nose into the
various rooms. As soon as she saw Daisy she started to
speak. The play-rooms were a disgrace, she had found
several broken crayons on the floor and there were
splodges of Play-Doh under one of the tables. 'And here
it is, half-past eight, and all of you late again.'

'I'm here,' Daisy reminded her in a matter-of-fact
voice, and, since her employer sounded rather more bad-
tempered than usual, she added mendaciously, 'and I
passed Mandy and Joyce as I came along the road.'

'It is a fortunate thing for you girls that I'm a tolerant
employer,' observed Mrs Gower-Jones peevishly. 'I see
that you'll have to make the place fit to be seen before
the children get here.'

She swept away to the nicely appointed room where
she interviewed parents and spent a good deal of the day
'doing the paperwork', as she called it, but Daisy, going
in hurriedly one day over some minor emergency, had
been in time to see the *Tatler* lying open on the desk,
and she was of the opinion that the paperwork didn't
amount to much.

The children started to arrive, a thin trickle at first
with time to bid a leisurely goodbye to mothers or
nannies and later, almost late, barely stopping to bid
farewell to their guardians, running into the cloakroom,
tossing their small garments and satchels all over the
place and bickering with each other. Mondays were never
good days, thought Daisy, coaxing a furious small boy
to hand over an even smaller girl's satchel.

The morning began badly and the day got worse. The cook, a local girl who saw to the dinners for the children, didn't turn up. Instead her mother telephoned to say that she had appendicitis and was to go into hospital at once.

Daisy, patiently superintending the messy pleasures of Play-Doh, was surprised when Mrs Gower-Jones came unexpectedly through the door and demanded her attention.

'Can you cook, Miss Pelham?' she wanted to know urgently.

'Well, yes—nothing fancy, though, Mrs Gower-Jones.' Daisy removed a lump of dough from a small girl's hair and returned it to the bowl.

'Mandy and Joyce say they can't,' observed Mrs Gower-Jones, crossly, 'so it will have to be you. The cook's had to go to hospital—I must say it's most inconsiderate of her. The children must have their dinners.'

'You want me to cook it?' asked Daisy calmly. 'But who is to look after the children? I can't be in two places at once.'

'I'll stay with them. For heaven's sake go along to the kitchen and get started; the daily girl's there, and she can do the potatoes and so on...'

Daisy reflected that if she were her employer she would very much prefer to cook the dinner than oversee a bunch of rather naughty children, but she didn't voice her thought, merely handed Mrs Gower-Jones her apron, advised her that the children would need to be cleaned up before their dinners and took herself off to the kitchen.

Marlene, the daily help, was standing by the kitchen table, doing nothing. Daisy wished her good morning,

suggested that she might put the kettle on and make a
cup of tea and said that she had come to cook the dinner.
Marlene, roused from daydreaming, did as she was
asked, volunteered to peel the potatoes and the carrots
and then observed that the minced meat had just been
delivered.

'Beefburgers,' said Daisy; mince, offered as such,
never went down well—perhaps the beefburgers would.
Marlene, brought to life by a mug of tea, saw to the
potatoes and carrots and began to collect cutlery ready
to lay the tables. Daisy, her small nose in and out of
store cupboards, added this and that to the mince,
thumped it into shape, rolled it out and cut it into circles
with one of Mrs Gower-Jones's best wine glasses, since
there was nothing else handy. She would have liked to
do chips but there wasn't time, so she puréed the potatoes with a generous dollop of butter and glazed the
carrots. By half-past twelve she was ready to dish up.

Mrs Gower-Jones took over then, drawing hissing
breaths at the nicely browned beefburgers and the
mounds of buttery potatoes. 'And really,' she protested
crossly, 'there is no need to put parsley on the carrots,
Miss Pelham.'

Which was all the thanks Daisy got.

There was a temporary cook the next day, an older
woman who spoke little English, and who, in Daisy's
opinion, didn't look quite clean. She served up fish
fingers and chips with tinned peas. Daisy thought that
she wasn't a cook at all but probably all Mrs Gower-
Jones could get at a moment's notice.

When she went into the kitchen the next morning to
fetch the children's mid-morning milk the sight of the

woman preparing dinner in a muddle of dirty sauce-
pans, potato peelings and unwashed dishes made her glad
that Mrs Gower-Jones's meanness stipulated that her assistants should bring their own lunches. Unwilling to
disparage a fellow worker, all the same she went in search
of her employer.

'The new cook seems to be in a bit of a muddle,' she
ventured. 'The kitchen . . .'

'Attend to your own work,' commanded Mrs Gower-
Jones. 'She is perfectly capable of attending to hers.'

The children ate their dinner—what Mrs Gower-Jones
described as a wholesome stew made from the best ingredients, followed by ice-cream—and Daisy, Mandy and
Joyce took it in turns to eat their own sandwiches before
arranging the children on their little camp beds for their
afternoon nap, a peaceful hour during which they prepared for the hour or so still left before the children were
collected. Only it wasn't peaceful; before the hour was
up every child—and there were forty of them—was
screaming his or her head off, clasping their small
stomachs in pain and being sick into the bargain.

Daisy, rousing Mrs Gower-Jones from the little nap
she took after lunch while the children were quiet, didn't
mince her words. 'All the children are vomiting and
worse—something they've eaten. They'll have to go to
hospital. I'll phone . . .'

She sped away to dial 999 and then to join the hard-
pressed Mandy and Joyce. The place was a shambles by
now and some of the children looked very ill. They wiped
hands and faces and comforted their wailing charges and
had no time for Mrs Gower-Jones, who had taken a look
and fled with her hands over her mouth, but she ap-

peared again when the first of the ambulances arrived, asserting her authority in a shrinking fashion.

'I shall have to notify the parents,' she uttered to no one in particular. 'Miss Pelham, go to the hospital and let me know immediately how the children are. Mandy, Joyce, you can stay here and clear up.'

It took some time to get all the children away; Daisy, squashed in with the last of them, looked down at herself. She smelt nasty for a start and the state of her overall bore witness to that fact; she felt hot and dirty and very worried. Food poisoning—she had no doubt that was what it was—was no light matter with small children; she remembered the new cook and shuddered.

Casualty was full of screaming children although some of them were too quiet. Daisy, making herself known without fuss, was led away to wash herself and remove the overall and then she was given a plastic apron to take its place. Feeling cleaner, she was handed over to a brisk young woman with an armful of admission slips and asked to name the children. It took quite a while for she stopped to comfort those who weren't feeling too bad and bawled to her to be taken home. The brisk young woman got a little impatient but Daisy, her kind heart torn by the miserable little white faces, wasn't to be hurried. The last two children were the twins, no longer difficult but greenish-white and lackadaisical, staring up at her in a manner so unlike their boisterous selves that she had a pang of fear. Disregarding her brisk companion's demand for their names, she bent over the trolley where they lay one at each end.

'You'll be all right very soon,' she assured them, and took limp little hands in hers. 'The doctor will come and make you well again...'

Two large hands calmly clasped her waist and lifted her to one side. 'He's here now,' said a voice in her ear and she looked up into the face of the owner of the Rolls-Royce.

Katie and Josh spoke as one. 'Uncle Valentine, my tummy hurts,' and Katie went even greener and gave an ominous heave. Daisy, a practical girl, held out her plastic apron and the man beside her said,

'Ah, sensible as well as sharp-tongued.' He looked over his shoulder. 'Staff Nurse, these two are dehydrated; get a drip up, will you? Dr Sims will see to it. Where's the child you told me couldn't stop vomiting? I'll see him next.' He patted the twins on their sweaty little heads, advised Daisy in a kindly voice to dispose of her apron as quickly as possible and, accompanied by one of the casualty sisters, went away, to disappear into the ordered chaos.

The brisk young woman showed her where to dump the apron, took a look at her overall and found her another plastic pinny. 'If I could have their names,' she said urgently. 'They called Dr Seymour Uncle Valentine...'

'Thorley, Katie and Josh, twins, almost four years old,' Daisy told her. 'They live along the Wylye valley— Steeple Langford, I believe. If I could see one of the sisters just for a minute perhaps she could let me know if any of the children are causing worry. Mrs Gower-Jones told me to phone her as soon as possible so that she can warn the parents.'

Her companion gave a snort. 'I should have thought it was Mrs whoever-it-is who should have come here with the children. Still, I'll see if I can find someone for you.'

A nurse and a young doctor had arrived as they talked and they began to set up the saline drips, no easy task for the twins took exception to this, screaming with rage and kicking and rolling round the trolley.

'Well, hold them still, will you?' begged the doctor impatiently. 'What a pair of little horrors...'

'Well, they don't feel well,' said Daisy with some spirit, 'and they're very small.' She leaned over the trolley, holding the wriggling children to her, talking to them in her quiet voice.

Dr Seymour, coming back to take another look, paused for a moment to admire the length of leg—Daisy had such nice legs, although no one had ever told her so. He said breezily, 'They need a ball and chain, although I have no doubt they prefer to have this young lady.' As Daisy resumed a more dignified position, he added, 'Thanks for your help—my nephew and niece are handfuls, are they not?' He ignored the young doctor's stare. 'You work at the nursery school? You may telephone the headmistress or whatever she is called and assure her that none of the children is in danger. I shall keep in some of the children for the night—Sister will give you their names. Run along now...'

Daisy, mild by nature, went pink. He had spoken to her as though she were one of the children and she gave him a cross look. If she had known how to toss her head she would have tossed it; as it was she said with a dignity which sat ill on her dishevelled appearance, 'I'm not at all surprised to know that the twins are your nephew and niece, Doctor.'

She gave him a small nod, smiled at the children and walked away; fortunately she didn't see his wide grin.

She was kept busy for quite some time; first getting a list of the children who would be staying for the night and then phoning Mrs Gower-Jones. That lady was in a cold rage; the nursery school would have to be closed down for the time being at least—her reputation would suffer—'and you will be out of a job,' she told Daisy nastily.

Daisy realised that her employer was battling with strong emotions. 'Yes, of course,' she said soothingly, 'but if you would just tell me what you want me to do next. Shall I stay until the children are collected?'

'Well of course,' said Mrs Gower-Jones ungratefully, 'I've enough to do here and Mandy and Joyce are still clearing up. I have never seen such a frightful mess; really, I should have thought you girls could have controlled the children.'

A remark which Daisy thought best not to answer.

She phoned her mother then went back to organise the children who would be fetched as soon as their parents had been told. Anxious mothers and nannies began arriving and in the ensuing chaos of handing over the children fit to go home Daisy lost count of time. They all, naturally enough, wanted to see Mrs Gower-Jones, and since she wasn't there several of them gave vent to their strong feelings, bombarding Daisy with questions and complaints. No matter that they had already had reassuring talks with Sister; they could hardly blame her for their children's discomfiture, but Daisy, unassuming and polite, was a splendid target for their indignation. She was battling patiently with the last of the mothers, a belligerent lady who appeared to think that Daisy was responsible for the entire unfortunate affair, when Dr Seymour loomed up beside her.

He had been there all the time, going to and fro with his houseman and registrar, making sure that the children were recovering, but Daisy had been too occupied to see him. Now he took the matter smoothly into his own hands.

'A most unfortunate thing to happen; luckily, none of the children is seriously affected.' He glanced down at the wan-faced small boy clutching his mother's hand. 'This little chap will be fine in a couple of days—Sister has told you what to do, I expect? This young lady is an assistant at the nursery school and is not to be blamed in any way. The matter will be investigated by the proper authorities but it is evident that the cause was either in the cooking or in the food. I suggest that you take the matter up with the principal of the school.'

Daisy, listening to this, reflected that he had a pleasant voice, deep and unhurried and just now with a hint of steel in it. Which might have accounted for the ungracious apology she received before the small boy was borne away.

'The last one?' asked the doctor.

'Yes. Only I'm not sure if I'm supposed to stay—there are the children who are to remain here for the night; their mothers are here but they might want to ask questions—the children's clothes and so on.'

'What's the telephone number of this nursery school?'

She told him, too tired to bother about why he wanted to know. She would have liked to go home but first she would have to go back and get her bike and very likely Mrs Gower-Jones would want a detailed account of what had transpired at the hospital. She yawned, and choked on it as Dr Seymour said from behind her, 'Mrs Gower-Jones is coming here—she should have been here in the first place. You will go home.' It was a statement, not a suggestion and he turned on his heel and then paused. 'How?'

'I have my bike at the school.' She hesitated. 'And my purse and things.'

'They'll be there in the morning; you can fetch them. The place will be closed as a nursery school at least for the time being. Did you come like that?'

She frowned. 'Yes.'

'I'll drive you to your home. Come along.'

Daisy, a mild girl, said, 'No, thank you,' with something of a snap. But that was a waste of time.

'Don't be silly,' advised Dr Seymour, and he caught her by the arm and marched her briskly out of the hospital and stuffed her into the Rolls while she was still thinking of the dignified reply she wished to make. No girl liked to be told she was silly.

'Where to?'

'Wilton.'

'Where in Wilton?'

'If you put me down by the market square...'

He sighed. 'Where in Wilton?'

'Box Cottage—on the way to Burcombe. But I can easily walk...'

He didn't bother to answer as he drove through the city streets and along the main road to Wilton. Once there, within minutes, he turned left at the crossroads by the market. 'Left or right?' he asked.

'On the left—the last cottage in this row.'

He slowed the car and stopped, and to her surprise got out to open her door. He opened the little garden gate too, which gave her mother time to get to the door.

'Darling, whatever has happened? You said the children were ill——' Mrs Pelham took in Daisy's appearance. 'Are you ill too? You look as though you've been sick...'

'Not me, the children, Mother, and I'm quite all right.' Since the doctor was towering over her she remembered her manners and introduced him.

'Dr Seymour very kindly gave me a lift.'

'How very kind of you.' Her mother smiled charmingly at him. 'Do come in and have a cup of coffee.'

He saw the look on Daisy's face and his thin mouth twitched. 'I must get back to the hospital, I'm afraid; perhaps another time?'

'Any time,' said Mrs Pelham largely, ignoring Daisy's frown. 'Do you live in Wilton? I don't remember seeing your car...?'

'In Salisbury, but I have a sister living along the Wylye valley.'

'Well, we don't want to keep you. Thank you for bringing Daisy home.' Mrs Pelham offered a hand but Daisy didn't. She had seen his lifted eyebrows at her name; Daisy was a silly name and it probably amused him. She wished him goodbye in a cool voice, echoing her mother's thanks. She didn't like him; he was overbearing and had ridden roughshod over her objections to being given a lift. That she would still have been biking tiredly from Salisbury without his offer was something she chose to ignore.

'What a nice man,' observed her mother as they watched the car sliding away, back to the crossroads. 'How very kind of him to bring you home. You must tell us all about it darling——' she wrinkled her nose '—but perhaps you'd like a bath first.'

When Daisy reached the nursery school in the morning she found Mrs Gower-Jones in a black mood. The cook had disappeared and the police were trying to trace her, she had had people inspecting her kitchen and asking questions and the school was to be closed until it had been thoroughly cleaned and inspected. A matter of some weeks, even months. 'So you can take a week's notice,' said Mrs Gower-Jones. 'I've seen the other girls too. Don't expect to come back here either; if and when I open again parents won't want to see any of you—they'll always suspect you.'

'I should have thought,' observed Daisy in a reasonable voice, 'that they would be more likely to suspect you, Mrs Gower-Jones. After all, you engaged the cook.'

Mrs Gower-Jones had always considered Daisy to be a quiet, easily put-upon girl; now she looked at her in amazement while her face slowly reddened. 'Well, really, Miss Pelham—how dare you say such a thing?'

'Well, it's true.' Dasiy added without rancour, 'Anyway I wouldn't want to come back here to work; I'd feel as suspicious as the parents.'

'Leave at once,' said her employer, 'and don't expect a reference. I'll post on your cheque.'

'I'll wait while you write it, Mrs Gower-Jones,' said Daisy mildly.

She was already making plans as she cycled back to Wilton. She would have to get another job as soon as possible; her mother's pension wasn't enough to keep all three of them and Pamela had at least two more years at school. They paid the estate a very modest rent but there were still taxes and lighting and heating and food. They relied on Daisy's wages to pay for clothes and small extra comforts. There was never any money to save; her father had left a few hundred pounds in the bank but that was for a rainy day, never to be spent unless in dire emergency.

Back home, she explained everything to her mother, carefully keeping any note of anxiety out of her voice. They would be able to go on much as usual for a week or two and surely in that time she would find a job. It was a pity she wasn't trained for anything; she had gone to a good school because her father had been alive then and the fees had been found, although at the cost of holidays and small luxuries, and since she had done well the plan had been to send her to one of the minor universities, leading to a teaching post eventually. His death had been unexpected and premature; Daisy left the university after only a year there and came home to shoulder the responsibilities of the household and take the job at the nursery school.

Her mother reassured, she went out and bought the local paper and searched the jobs column. There was nothing; at least, there was plenty of work for anyone who understood computers and the like and there were several pigpersons wanted, for pig breeding flourished in her part of the world. It was a great pity that the tourist season would be over soon, otherwise she might have enquired if there was work for her in the tearooms at Wilton House. Tomorrow, she decided, she would go into Salisbury, visit the agencies and the job centre.

It was a bad time of year to find work, she was told; now if she had asked when the season started, no doubt there would have been something for her—a remark kindly meant but of little comfort to her.

By the end of the week her optimism was wearing thin although she preserved a composed front towards her mother and Pamela. She was sitting at her mother's writing desk answering an advertisement for a mother's help when someone knocked on the door. Pamela was in her room, deep in schoolwork; her mother was out shopping. Daisy went to answer it.

CHAPTER TWO

DAISY recognised the person on the doorstep. 'Lady Thorley—please come in. The twins are all right?'

'Quite recovered,' said their mother. 'I wanted to talk to you...'

Daisy led the way into the small sitting-room, nicely furnished and with a bowl of roses on the Georgian circular table under the window, offered a chair and then sat down opposite her visitor, her hands folded quietly in her lap, composedly waiting to hear the reason for the visit. It would be something to do with the nursery school, she felt sure, some small garment missing...

'Are you out of a job?' Lady Thorley smiled. 'Forgive me for being nosy, but Mrs Gower-Jones tells me that she has closed the place down for some time at least.'

'Well, yes, she has, and we all had a week's notice...'

'Then if you are free, would you consider coming to us for a while? The twins—they're a handful, more than I can cope with, and they like you. If you hear of something better you would be free to go, but you would be a godsend. There must be other nursery schools, although I don't know of any. I thought that if you would come while I find a governess for them...only I don't want to be hurried over that—she will have to be someone rather special. Would you give it a try?'

'I could come each day?'

'Oh, yes. We're at Steeple Langford—about three miles from here. Is there a bus?'

'I have a bike.'

'You'll give it a try? Is half-past eight too early for you? Until five o'clock—that's a long day, I know, but you would have Saturday and Sunday.' She hesitated. 'And perhaps occasionally you would sleep in if we were about to go out for the evening? We have some good servants but I'd rather it was you.' And when Daisy hesitated she added, 'I don't know what you were paid by Mrs Gower-Jones but we would pay the usual rate.' She named a sum which sent Daisy's mousy eyebrows up. Twice the amount Mrs Gower-Jones had paid her; heaven-sent, although she felt bound to tell her visitor that it was more than she had earned at the nursery school.

'By the end of the week you will agree with me that you will have earned every penny. You have only had the twins for a few days, diluted with other children. Full-strength, as it were, they're formidable.' She smiled charmingly. 'You see, I'm not pretending that they're little angels. I love them dearly but because of that I'm not firm enough.'

'When would you like me to start?' asked Daisy. 'Only you'll want references.'

'Oh, never mind those,' said Lady Thorley breezily, 'Valentine told me that you were a sensible girl with an honest face and he's always right.'

Daisy blushed and Lady Thorley thought how pleasant it was to find a girl who still could, happily unaware that it wasn't a blush at all, just Daisy's temper, seldom roused, coming to the surface. Even if that was all he could think of to say about her, it would have been far better if he had kept quiet—honest and sensible indeed; what girl wanted to be called that?

For a moment she was tempted to change her mind and refuse the job, but then she remembered the marvellous wages... 'How kind,' she murmured, and agreed to cycle over to Steeple Langford the next morning.

Lady Thorley went presently and Daisy tore up her reply to the advertisement for a home help and then did cautious sums on the back of the writing paper. The job wouldn't last forever—a month, six weeks perhaps—but the money would take care of the phone bill and the gas and electricity as well. There would be enough left over for her mother to have a pair of good shoes ready for the winter, and Pamela to have another of the baggy sweaters she craved, and she herself—Daisy sucked the end of her pen—torn between high-heeled elegant shoes she would probably never have the chance to wear and a pair of sensible boots; last winter's pair had had their day and were beyond repair. She was still brooding over this when her mother and Pamela came back, and, much heartened by the news, Mrs Pelham fetched the bottle of sherry they hoarded for special occasions and they all had a glass. 'I mustn't forget Razor,' said Daisy. 'I'll get some of that luxury catfood he enjoys and perhaps a tin of sardines.'

The road along the Wylye was quiet, used mainly by local people, winding from one small village to the next one with glimpses of the river from time to time and plenty of trees. It was a splendid morning and Daisy cycled along it trying to guess what the job would turn out to be. Hard work, no doubt, but the money was good...

The Thorleys' house was on the further side of Steeple Langford, a roomy place typical of the area, with plenty of large windows, a veranda and a wide porch. It was surrounded by nicely laid-out grounds with plenty of trees and as she went up the short drive she could see ponies and a donkey in the small adjoining field.

The front door was opened as she reached it and the two children and a black Labrador dog spilled out noisily. Daisy got off her bike. 'Hello,' she said cheerfully, 'what's your dog's name?'

'Boots. Have you got a dog?' They had crowded round her, all three of them.

'No, though we had one when I was a little girl. We have a cat; he's called Razor.'

'Why?'

'He's very sharp...'

The twins hooted with mirth. 'May we see him?'

'Perhaps one day your mother will let you come and see him. We'll see.'

'Why do all grown-ups say "we'll see"?'

Daisy was saved from answering this by the appearance of Lady Thorley, wearing the kind of thin jersey dress that Daisy coveted.

'Good morning. May we call you Daisy? Come on inside and have a look round. We've just finished breakfast but there's coffee if you'd like it.'

Daisy declined the coffee, propped her bike against the porch and, with a twin on either side of her, went into the house.

It was as nice inside as it was out; comfortably furnished with some good pieces, a great many comfortable chairs, flowers everywhere and a slight untidiness which one would expect in a house where there were children and dogs. The nursery was on the first floor overlooking the back lawn, a large room with a low shelf around its walls to accommodate the various toys the twins possessed. There was a low table too and small chairs and also a comfortable chair or two for grown-ups.

'They prefer to be out of doors,' said their mother. 'They're very energetic, I'm afraid. I'll show you the garden and then leave you, shall I?' She led the way downstairs again. 'The children have their milk about half-past ten and Jenny will bring your coffee at the same time. They have their lunch just after twelve, with me—and you, of course—and they have their tea at five o'clock before bed at six o'clock.' Lady Thorley hesitated. 'I'm sometimes out to lunch...' She looked doubtfully at Daisy.

'I'm sure Josh and Katie will keep me company when you are,' said Daisy matter-of-factly and watched their mother's face light up with relief.

'The children had a nanny until quite recently,' confided Lady Thorley. 'She—she was very strict.'

'I don't know if I'm strict or not,' said Daisy cheerfully. She beamed down at the children. 'We'll have to find out, won't we?'

She spent the rest of the morning in the garden with the twins and Boots, pausing only long enough to drink her coffee while they reluctantly drank their milk. At lunch they were difficult, picking at their food, casting sly glances at their mother as they spilt their drinks, kicked the rungs of their chairs and upset the salt cellar. Lady Thorley said helplessly, 'Darlings, do behave yourselves.' She spoke in a loving voice which held no authority at all and they took no notice of her.

'I wonder,' observed Daisy pleasantly, 'if it would be a good idea, Lady Thorley, if Josh and Katie were to have their lunch in the nursery for a few days—by themselves, of course...? I'll sit in the room with them, naturally.'

Lady Thorley caught Daisy's look. 'What a good idea,' she said enthusiastically. 'Why didn't I think of it before? We'll start tomorrow.'

The twins exchanged glances. 'Don't want to,' said Josh, and was echoed by Katie. They had stuck their small lower lips out, ready to be mutinous.

'Well,' said Daisy, 'if you really don't want to, will you eat your lunch like grown-up people with your mother and me?'

'You're strict...'

'Not a bit of it. While you're having your rest I'll read whatever story you want.'

It had seemed a long day, thought Daisy as she cycled back home, but she had enjoyed it. The twins were nice children, spoilt by their mother and probably too strictly brought up by the nanny. She began to plan a daily regime which might, at least in part, correct some of that. They were very bright for their age; she would have to win their confidence as well as their liking.

By the end of the week she felt reasonably sure that she had done that; the twins were about the naughtiest children she had had to deal with while she had worked for Mrs Gower-Jones, and so charming with their large blue eyes and innocent little faces that it was sometimes difficult to be firm, but they seemed to like her and since she ignored their small tantrums she felt that she was making progress. She liked the job too, and enjoyed the cycle ride each day and the long hours spent out of doors with the children. The weather was delightful too, dry and warm with no hint of autumn. Of course, the ride wouldn't be so nice in rain and wind, but she would be gone by then, although Lady Thorley hadn't mentioned the likelihood of a governess yet.

Lady Thorley was going out to lunch, Daisy remembered as she pedalled along the quiet road, and since it was such a fine day perhaps she and the twins could have a picnic in the garden; she was good friends with the cook and the elderly housemaid and surely between them they could concoct a picnic instead of the usual meal indoors.

The twins were waiting for her with faithful Boots and she went up to the nursery with them for an hour's playschool—Plasticine and wooden blocks, crayons and large sheets of scribbling paper—and they were tidying up when their mother came to say that she was going out to her lunch party and would be back by teatime. She looked elegant and pretty and Daisy had no doubt in her mind that her husband must adore her. The twins were kissed and told to be good, and Daisy was to be sure and ask for anything she might want. The three of them escorted her to the door and waved as she drove away in her smart little Mini, and Katie began to sniff sorrowfully.

'Who's coming to help get our picnic ready?' asked Daisy, and whisked the moppet out into the garden with

Josh and Boots. 'Look, Cook's put a table ready; let's put the plates and knives and things on it and then we'll go to the kitchen and fetch the food.'

She was leading the way back to the garden, laden with a tray of dishes—hard-boiled eggs, bacon sandwiches, little sausages on sticks and a mushroom quiche—when she saw Dr Seymour sitting on the grass leaning against the table. The children had seen him too; the dish of apples Josh had been carrying went tumbling to the ground and Katie, close behind him, dropped the plastic mugs she held as they galloped towards him with shrieks of delight. He uncoiled his vast person in one neat movement and received their onslaught with lazy good humour. 'May I stay to lunch?' he asked Daisy and, since he quite obviously intended to anyway, she said politely,

'Of course, Dr Seymour. Lady Thorley is out but she'll be back at teatime.' She put down her tray. 'I'll fetch the rest of the food...'

She started back to the house and found him beside her, trailed by the twins and Boots. 'Quite happy here?' he wanted to know.

'Yes, thank you.'

'Pleased to see me again?'

What an outrageous man, thought Daisy, and what a colossal conceit. She said pleasantly, 'Should I be, Dr Seymour?'

'Upon reflection, perhaps not.' They had reached the kitchen and found Cook, who had seen his car, cutting a mound of beef sandwiches. 'You'll be peckish, sir,' she said comfortably. 'Hard-boiled eggs and sausages on sticks aren't hardly fitting for a gentleman of your size, if you don't mind me saying it.'

He took a sandwich and bit into it. 'When have I ever disputed an opinion of yours, Mrs Betts? And if I can't finish them I'm sure Daisy will help me out.'

So she was Daisy, was she? And she had no intention of eating his beef sandwiches. She didn't say so although she gave him a chilly look.

It was impossible to remain chilly for long; the twins, on their best behaviour because their favourite uncle was going to share their picnic, saw to that. The meal was an unqualified success; Josh ate everything he was offered and, since Katie always did as he did, the usual patient battle to get them to eat didn't take place; instead, the doctor kept them entertained with a mixture of mild teasing and ridiculous stories in the face of which it was impossible to remain stand-offish; indeed Daisy enjoyed herself and found herself forgetting how much she disapproved of him. That was until he remarked, as the last of the lemonade was being drunk, 'I hope Meg has got you on a long lease.'

She gave him a puzzled look. 'A long lease . . . ?'

'It would seem to me that you have all the makings of a family nanny, handed down from one generation to another.'

Daisy, a mild-tempered girl, choked back rage. 'I have no intention of being anything of the sort.' Her pleasant voice held a decidedly acid note.

'No? Planning to get married?'

'No, and if I may say so, Dr Seymour, I must remind you that it's none of your business.'

'No, no, of course it isn't; put it down to idle curiosity.'

Josh, for nearly four years old, was very bright. 'You're not married either, Uncle Val; I know 'cos Mummy said it was high time and it was time you thought about it.'

His uncle ate a last sandwich. 'Mummy's quite right; I must think about it.'

Daisy began to collect up the remains of their meal. 'Everyone carry something,' ordered the doctor, 'and no dropping it on the way to the kitchen. What happens next?' He looked at Daisy.

'They rest for an hour—I read to them.'

'Oh, good. I could do with a nap myself. We can all fit into the hammock easily enough—not you, of course, Daisy. What gem of literature are you reading at the moment?'

'Grimm's fairy-tales; they choose a different story each day.'

She wasn't sure how to reply to the doctor's remarks; she suspected that he was making fun of her, not unkindly but perhaps to amuse himself. Well, she had no intention of letting him annoy her. 'Perhaps you would like to choose?' she asked him as, the picnic cleared away, they crossed the lawn to where the hammock stood under the shade of the trees.

He arranged a padded chair for her before lying back in the hammock with the twins crushed on either side of him. ' "Faithful John",' he told her promptly.

She opened the book. 'It's rather long,' she said doubtfully.

'I dare say we shall all be asleep long before you've finished.'

He closed his eyes and the children lay quietly; there was nothing for it but to begin.

He had been right; Josh dropped off first and then Katie, and since he hadn't opened his eyes she supposed that the doctor had gone to sleep too. She closed the book on its bookmark, kicked off her sandals and sat back against the cushions. They might sleep for half an hour and she had plenty to occupy her thoughts.

Dr Seymour opened one eye. He said very softly, 'You don't like me very much, do you, Daisy?'

She was taken by surprise, but Daisy being Daisy she gave his remark thoughtful consideration. Presently she said, 'I don't know anything about you, Dr Seymour.'

'An indisputable fact. You haven't answered my question.'

'Yes, I have—I don't know you well enough to know, do I?'

'No? Personally, I know if I like or dislike someone the moment I set eyes on them.'

He would have disliked her on sight, she reflected, remembering the cold stare at the traffic-lights in Wilton and the short shrift he had given her, almost knocking her off her bike. She said primly, 'Well, we're all different, aren't we?'

The mocking look he gave her sent the colour into her cheeks. The doctor, watching her lazily, decided that she wasn't as plain as he had thought.

The twins woke up presently and they played ball until their mother came back. The twins fell upon her with shrieks of delight, both talking at once. 'Val—how lovely to see you—I wanted to talk to you...' Seeing Daisy, she turned to her. 'Do go home, dear, you must be exhausted—I know I am after several hours of these two.' She unwound her children's arms from around her neck. 'Take Daisy to the gate, darlings, and then go to the kitchen and ask Mrs Betts if she would make a pot of tea for me.'

Daisy got to her feet, reflecting that Lady Thorley's airy dismissal had been both friendly and expected; she was the daily mother's help and was treated with more consideration than she had ever had with Mrs Gower-Jones. All the same, she wished that Dr Seymour hadn't been there.

Her goodnight was quietly said. 'I'll be here at half-past eight, Lady Thorley,' and she left them without further ado, taking the twins with her.

The doctor watched her go. 'What do you want to tell me, Meg?' he asked.

'Hugh phoned—such news—the man at the Hague is ill—jaundice or something—and he's to replace him until he's fit again. Hugh says there's a lovely flat we can have and he wants us to go there with him—he'll be home this evening but I wanted to ask your advice about the twins. I'll go with Hugh, of course, but what about them? I did wonder if they had better stay here with Daisy—that is if she would agree to come...'

'Why not take the children with you and Daisy as well?'

'Well, that would be marvellous—she's so good with them and they like her, but she might not want to come...'

'Why not ask her and find out? What does Hugh say?'

'He told me I could do whatever I thought was best as long as it won't upset the twins—going to live somewhere else—foreign too...'

'My dear girl, Holland is hardly darkest Africa, and it's only an hour away by plane.' He stood up. 'I must go back to town. You're quite satisfied with Daisy?'

'Oh, yes. How clever of you to tell me about her, Val. She's so sensible and kind—it's hard to find girls like her. Plain, of course—such a pity for she'd make a splendid wife.' She walked round the house to where his car was parked before the door. 'I suppose you wouldn't find the time to visit us while we're at the Hague?'

'Very likely—I'm lecturing at Leiden Medical School and there's a seminar for paediatricians in Utrecht—I'm not sure of the dates.' Lady Thorley tiptoed to kiss his cheek.

'Lovely. I'll talk to Daisy—better still I'll get Hugh to do that.'

'Why not? When does he go?'

'Two weeks—at least, he's to go as soon as possible; he thought it would take me two weeks to pack up and so on.' She stopped suddenly. 'Oh, what shall I do about Boots? We can't leave him here just with Mrs Betts...'

'I'll have him.' He glanced at his watch. 'I must go, my dear—give me a ring when you have things settled.'

Daisy, unaware of the future being mapped out for her, cycled home and thought about Dr Seymour. She wasn't sure if she liked him but she was fair enough to admit that that was because he was a difficult man to get to know. He was splendid with the children, probably he was an excellent paediatrician, but he was arrogant and, she suspected, used to having his own way. Moreover, he had this nasty habit of mocking her...

She was surprised to find Sir Hugh at home when she reached Steeple Langford the next morning. He was still young but he had a serious manner which made him seem older.

'If we might talk?' he suggested, coming to the nursery where the twins were running riot with the Plasticine under Daisy's tolerant eye.

Daisy's heart sank. He had come to tell her she was no longer needed, a governess had been found, and she was mentally putting her name down at several agencies in Salisbury when he went on. 'I'm about to be posted to Den Haag for a time; we wondered if you would consider coming with us to look after the children? I'm not sure for how long; I'm to fill in for a colleague who's on sick leave.'

'Me?' said Daisy.

'If you would. We're to take over an apartment in the residential part of the city, with a garden, I believe, and there are parks close by, so I'm told, and of course it is close to the sea.'

'I don't speak Dutch,' said Daisy.

He smiled faintly. 'Nor do I. I believe that almost everyone speaks English—there are certainly a good many English people living there—there would be other children for the twins to play with, and I'm sure there are young Englishwomen living there—you wouldn't be lonely.' When she hesitated he added, 'I'm told it will be for a month or six weeks.'

'If I might have time to talk to my mother? I could let you know in the morning if that would do?'

'Certainly, I shall be here for a good part of tomorrow.' He got up. 'My wife and I do so hope that you'll see your way to coming with us! You'll let me know in the morning?'

'Yes, Sir Hugh. For my part I should like to come, but I must tell my mother first.'

She thought about it a good deal during the day with mounting excitement; it would mean that she was sure of the job for at least another month besides the added pleasure of seeing something of another country. She would have to talk to Pam and make sure that she could cope with the various household demands. She wouldn't be able to add to the housekeeping money each week while she was away, but there was enough in the bank to cover them and she could pay that back when she eventually returned. All in all she was sure that everything could be arranged with the minimum of trouble for her mother and sister.

Her news was received with pleased surprise; there was no doubt at all, declared her mother, that they could manage very well while she was away. 'It's a marvellous opportunity,' said Mrs Pelham happily. 'Who knows who you will meet while you are there?' she added enthusiastically. 'Sir Hugh is something to do with the Foreign Office, isn't he? There must be clerks and people...'

Daisy said, 'Yes, Mother, I'm sure there are.' There was no harm in letting her mother daydream. Daisy, well aware of her commonplace features and retiring disposition, thought it unlikely that even the most lowly clerk would give her as much as a second glance.

Not a girl to give way to self-pity, she spent the evening combing through her wardrobe in search of suitable clothes. The result was meagre; it was Pamela who remembered the raspberry-red brocade curtains some aunt or other had bequeathed to their mother. They were almost new; they spread them out on the sitting-room floor and studied them. 'A skirt,' said Pamela. 'We'll get a good pattern, and Mother—there's that white crêpe de Chine blouse with the wide collar you never wear.'

'But will I need them?' asked Daisy doubtfully.

'Perhaps not, but you must have something, just in case you get asked out. There's your good suit and we can get your raincoat cleaned...'

So when Daisy saw Sir Hugh in the morning she told him that she would go to Den Haag with the twins, and was rather touched by his relief. His wife's relief was even more marked. 'I hardly slept,' she told Daisy, 'wondering what we should do if you decided not to come with us; Josh and Katie will be so happy. I should warn you that I shall have to be out a good deal—there's a lot of social life, Hugh tells me—you won't mind, will you?'

Daisy assured her that she didn't mind in the least and Lady Thorley gave a sigh of relief. 'You'll have a day off each week, of course, though I dare say it will have to be on different days, and an hour or two to yourself each day. Hugh wants us to go in ten days' time. We'll see to the travel arrangements, of course. There's just your luggage and passport.' She smiled widely. 'I think it's going to be great fun.'

Daisy agreed with her usual calm. Looking after the twins wasn't exactly fun; she liked doing it but it was tiring and keeping the upper hand over two small children determined to be disobedient was taxing both to temper and patience. But she truly liked Lady Thorley, and the twins, naughty though they were, had stolen her affection.

It was impossible not to be excited as preparations got under way for their journey: clothes for the twins, their favourite toys carefully packed, and a good deal of over-time because their mother needed to go to London to shop for herself. Daisy assembled her own modest wardrobe, wrapped the crêpe de Chine blouse in tissue paper, dealt with the household bills and with Pamela's help made quite a good job of the skirt. Trying it on finally and eyeing it critically, she decided that anyone not knowing that it had been a curtain would never guess...

It wanted two days to their departure when Dr Seymour turned up again. Lady Thorley was packing and Daisy and the twins, housebound by a sudden bout of heavy rain, were in the nursery. He came in so silently that none of them was aware of him until he spoke in Daisy's ear.

'An artist as well as a nanny?' he wanted to know, studying the variety of drawings on the paper before her.

Her pencil faltered so that the rabbit's ear that she had been sketching didn't look in the least like an ear. She said evenly, 'Good afternoon, Dr Seymour,' and rubbed out the ear while Josh and Katie rushed at their uncle.

He pulled a chair up beside Daisy, picked up a pencil and added a moustache and beard to the rabbit.

'Ready to go?' he asked her.

'Yes, thank you. Would you like me to fetch Lady Thorley?'

'No. I came to see these two. Being good, are they? Not turning your mousy locks grey or causing you to lose weight?'

How could he know that she detested her soft brown hair and was shy about her slightly plump person? A good thing she wouldn't see him for at least six weeks for she didn't like him.

'No,' said Daisy, 'they're good children.' Which wasn't in the least true but Katie, hearing it, flung her arms round her neck.

'We love Daisy; we think she is beautiful and kind like a princess in a fairy-tale waiting for the prince to come and rescue her.'

'And why not?' said her uncle idly, getting up from his chair. 'I'm going to see your mother but I'll say goodbye before I go.'

Josh climbed on to a chair beside her. 'Draw a bear,' he ordered. 'I'm going to be just like Uncle Val when I grow up.'

'So am I,' said Katie, and was told not to be a silly little girl by her brother. Threatened tears were averted by Daisy's embarking on a description of the party dress Katie, being a girl, would be able to wear when she was grown up.

Josh curled his small lip. 'Girls,' he said scornfully.

The doctor was still there when Daisy went home; she cycled past his car in the drive, unaware that he was watching her from the drawing-room window.

Two days later she said goodbye to her mother and Pamela, gave Razor a cuddle and went to the gate where Lady Thorley and the twins were waiting in their car. Her case was stowed in the boot and she got in the back with the children. They were strangely subdued and their mother said, 'Val came for Boots last night and they miss him—he's to stay with my brother while we're away.'

So Daisy spent a good part of their journey explaining how very much Boots would enjoy a holiday. 'And think of all the things you can tell him when we get back,' she pointed out.

'We wouldn't let anyone else have him, only Uncle Val,' said Katie tearfully.

'Well, of course not. He's family, isn't he? And Boots knows that he belongs to all the family as well as you two. You might send him a postcard from Holland...'

A suggestion which did much to cheer the children up.

Sir Hugh had made sure that his family need have no worries on their journey. They were met at Gatwick, the car was garaged and they were guided through the business of checking tickets, baggage and Customs and seen safely aboard the plane. The children were a little peevish by now and Daisy was relieved to see lemonade and biscuits and, for herself, coffee.

Lady Thorley was on the other side of the aisle and the first-class compartment was only half-full; Daisy drank her coffee while the twins munched and swallowed, grateful for the short respite. Afterwards there were comics to be looked at and the excitement of visiting the toilets, small enough at the best of times but needing a good deal of side-stepping and squeezing, much to the delight of the children.

By then the plane was coming in to land, something the twins weren't quite sure if they liked or not. Daisy wasn't sure if she liked it or not herself.

They were met by a well turned-out chauffeur at Schiphol and shepherded through Customs and into a gleaming, rather old-fashioned car and driven away. A little over an hour's drive, the chauffeur told them, joining the stream of traffic.

The twins, one on each side of their mother, on the back seat, stared out of the windows and had little to say beyond excited 'oh's and 'ah's. Daisy, sitting beside the chauffeur, gazed her fill too; she mustn't miss anything for she had promised to write every detail to her mother.

Presently the car left the busy streets around the airport and picked up speed along the motorway. There wasn't much to see here—occasional patches of quiet meadows, but it seemed to her that there were a great many factories lining the road and she felt vague disappointment. Not for long, however; soon the factories dwindled and died away to be replaced by trees and charming houses, set well back from the road which in turn gave way to the outskirts of the city.

The streets were busy here and the chauffeur had to slow down, so that she had a chance to look around her. It looked delightful—old gabled houses, canals, imposing buildings, a splendid place to explore on her free days... They left the heart of the city, driving down a straight road with parks on either side and then large, solid houses, set well apart from each other, before they turned off into a side-road, wide and tree-lined. There were blocks of modern flats on either side and here and there town mansions in their own grounds. Halfway down they stopped before the wide entrance of a solid red-brick block of flats and the chauffeur got out, opened their doors and led the way across the pavement as a concierge came hurrying to meet them.

'I do hope,' said Lady Thorley, 'that someone has put the kettle on; we need a cup of tea.' She smiled at Daisy, 'You must be tired; I know I am.'

Daisy had the twins by the hand, dancing with excitement. She thought it unlikely that she would have time to be tired until they were given their tea and put to bed, but that didn't worry her. 'I'd love one,' she said cheerfully.

CHAPTER THREE

THE concierge led them inside, across a wide hall to an ornate lift. She was a tall, bony woman with a hooked nose and a cast in one eye and the twins stared at her with growing delight. 'Is—is she a——?' began Josh.

'No, dear,' began Daisy before he could utter the word, 'this is the lady who looks after these flats...'

'Juffrouw Smit.' She ushered them into the lift which took them to the first floor. The landing was as wide as the hall below with a door on either side, one of which she now opened. 'The apartment,' she announced, and ushered them inside.

The flat was large, with lofty ceilings, large windows and a balcony overlooking a sizeable garden. There was a staircase at one end of it leading to the garden and Juffrouw Smit waved a generous arm. 'It is yours, the garden.'

'Oh, how nice,' said Lady Thorley uncertainly. 'The people in the flat below?'

Juffrouw Smit shrugged. 'A very small apartment; he is but a clerk.'

Daisy peered over the balcony balustrade. There were iron railings separating the flat from the garden; it seemed hard on its occupant.

It was obvious that Juffrouw Smit was preparing another speech in her very basic English. 'The cook and the serving maid wait in the kitchen.'

She led the way through two handsome reception-rooms, a small sitting-room and down a short passage and opened a door.

The kitchen was a good size and, as far as Daisy could see at a glance, well equipped. There were two women there, stoutly built and well past their first youth, with pleasant round faces and white aprons over dark dresses. They smiled and nodded, shook hands and said, 'Welcome,' several times. The elder of them pointed to herself. 'Mien,' she said and then pointed to her companion and said, 'Corrie—we speak English a little and understand.'

She beamed at everyone. 'I make tea? I make good English tea . . .'

'Oh, splendid,' said Lady Thorley. 'Please—in the sitting-room?' She turned to Juffrouw Smit. 'Thank you for your help.'

'At your service, Lady Thorley. I will help at any time.'

She stalked away and Lady Thorley said, 'Well, we'd better go to the sitting-room and have tea and then we can get unpacked. Hugh will be here soon. Daisy, I shall leave you to see about the children's suppers and get them to bed. I must say this is rather a nice flat. You like your room?'

Daisy had had no time to more than glance at it; it was next to the children's room and what she supposed would be the play-room while they were there. There was a bathroom too; all were tucked away at the end of a passage at one end of the flat. She said now, 'It seemed very nice and the twins' room is a nice size.'

'Oh, good.' They were all in the sitting-room now, a comfortably furnished room obviously meant for family use, and Lady Thorley was leafing through the little pile of envelopes on the small desk under the window. 'Heavens, invitations already; I only hope I've brought the right clothes with me...'

They had their tea while the children drank their milk and presently Daisy took them with her to do the unpacking, a lengthy business as they wanted to help, and by the time it was done and she had put away her own modest wardrobe it was almost bedtime for them. There was no sign of Lady Thorley although there was a distant murmur of voices from the other end of the flat. Daisy, with a twin on either hand, found her way to the kitchen.

Mien was at a table putting the finishing touches to a salad.

'Could the children have supper?' Daisy asked.

'You tell, I make,' said Mien obligingly.

'Milk?' She glanced at the twins who were scowling horribly. 'Buttered toast?' she suggested. 'Coddled eggs? Yoghurt?'

She was rewarded by Josh's glare. 'Noodles—buttered noodles?' Daisy asked hopefully and saw Mien nod. 'These I have, with buttered toast and a special sauce. In fifteen minutes, miss, it will be brought to you in the play-room.'

Daisy heaved a sigh of relief. Mien's English was excellent; her accent was terrible but who cared about that? She smiled widely at the cook, went back to the children's room and got them ready for bed. They had had their baths and were cosily wrapped in their dressing-gowns when their supper was put before them.

The play-room had a door on to the balcony; moreover it boasted a piano, several small comfortable chairs and several shelves and cupboards. The children were hungry and the noodles were almost finished when their parents came in.

'Daisy, how clever of you. The children look at home already. How did you make Cook understand?'

'She speaks good English and is so helpful. The children are ready for bed when they've finished their supper; I thought an early night...'

'Quite right. As soon as you've tucked them up come to the sitting-room and we will have dinner.' The Thorleys stayed for a while, talking to the children, and presently went away, leaving Daisy to coax them to their beds. They were disposed to be fretful but she tucked them in firmly, picked up a book and sat between their beds until they slept and then went away to tidy herself for dinner.

Her room was small but comfortably furnished and the bathroom she was to share with the twins was more than adequate. She did her face and hair, changed her dress and went along to the sitting-room.

'We thought we would dine here this evening,' said Lady Thorley, 'as it's just the three of us. Hugh says that we shall entertain a lot, Daisy, so you won't mind if you have your dinner in the play-room from time to time?'

'Not at all,' said Daisy. 'I'm quite happy to have it there every evening. It's near the children if they should wake, too.'

Lady Thorley looked relieved. 'You wouldn't mind? You will have lunch with me, of course, unless there are guests. Now, we have to decide your free time too.'

Of which there was none, it seemed, during the day, although she was free to take the children out to the beach at Scheveningen whenever she wished. There was a car with a driver she might use if Lady Thorley wasn't free to drive them, and there was a park close by where she would meet other English girls and could chat while the children played together. 'You must have one day a week to yourself,' declared Lady Thorley. 'One of Hugh's colleagues has a nanny who is free on Wednesdays and he suggests that his wife and I should join forces and take it in turns to spend the day at each other's houses with all the children. If you would get the children up and dressed I'll see to their breakfasts and there is no need for you to come back until late evening.' She added apologetically, 'I know that compared with other jobs, you won't get much free time, but you can arrange your days to suit yourself, as long as I know where you are. The children will love the beach... Oh, and some Sundays we'll take the children out and you will be able to go to church...'

'Thank you, that sounds fine, Lady Thorley, and I'll let you know each day where we shall be going. The twins love to walk and there'll be a lot to see.'

She drank her coffee and excused herself on the plea that she would like to write home...

'There's a phone in the lobby leading off the hall,' said Sir Hugh. 'Telephone your mother now and there won't be such an urgent need to write at once.'

It was a temptation to have a good gossip with her mother and Pamela but she confined her news to the fact that they had arrived safely and that everything was quite perfect, promised to write as soon as possible and took herself off to bed.

The Thorleys were still in the sitting-room with the door half-open. As she went past, Lady Thorley's rather high voice reached her clearly. 'Val's coming over quite soon. There's heaps of room for him to stay here; we must invite some people to meet him...'

Daisy, getting ready for bed, allowed her thoughts to wander. She wasn't sure if she wanted to meet Dr Seymour again; on the other hand she had to admit that she found him interesting. Not, she reflected, that she was likely to have much to do with him even if he was a guest in the flat; she could see that any social life she might see would be from the outside looking in. Not that she minded, she told herself stoutly and, being a sensible girl, went to sleep at once.

The next day was largely taken up with finding their way around. They went into the garden after breakfast and then walked to the nearby park, although there wasn't time to do more than give it a brief visit before they went back to have their lunch with Lady Thorley; and, since they were nicely tired by now, the twins consented to lie down for a while, giving Daisy a chance to get her letter home started. In the afternoon they went out again, this time to watch the trams at the end of the road. These went to Scheveningen and back and Daisy decided that going to the beach by tram might be much more fun than driving there in a car. She would have to ask Sir Hugh if that was allowed. Tucking the children in that evening, she considered that their first day had been quite successful. The twins were taking everything in their stride, Mien produced exactly the right food for them and Corrie hadn't seemed to mind the extra work when Daisy had asked if she might have her dinner in the play-room. Perhaps there had been a nanny before her and it was the normal thing to do.

They spent most of the next day at Scheveningen, driven there by a morose man from the British embassy and collected by him during the afternoon. Daisy's request that they might use the trams had been received by Sir Hugh with sympathy, but he wished to take advice from his colleagues first... All the same, they had a lovely day. The sand stretched as far as the eye could see in either direction and there was a great deal of it. They built sandcastles, paddled in the rather chilly water and ate a splendid lunch of sandwiches and buns and potato crisps and went very willingly to bed when they were home again. Lady Thorley had joined them for nursery tea. 'Such a busy day,' she had declared. 'I would have liked to be on the beach with you. You must be tired, Daisy. We're going out to dinner this evening, but when you have had yours, do watch television in the sitting-room or go into the garden for an hour.'

It was a splendid evening, the first hint of autumn in its creeping dusk and faint chill, much too nice to sit and watch an indifferent TV programme which she couldn't understand anyway. The twins already asleep and her dinner eaten, Daisy pulled a cardigan around her shoulders and went down the staircase to the garden. The sun had set but the wide sky reflected its rays still and the garden, carefully tended, smelled faintly of lavender and pinks with the faintest whiff of roses along the end wall. She wandered along its length and then back again to be brought up short by a voice from behind the iron railings before the ground floor apartment.

'I saw you yesterday but you had the children with you.' A cheerful face peered at her through the bars. 'Philip Keynes—I live here. It's a very small flat but I'm a clerk at the embassy and on my own. It's nice to have someone in the flat above... Are you a daughter?'

'Me? No. I'm a temporary nanny—Daisy Pelham—just until they can find a governess for Josh and Katie.'

They faced each other through the bars, liking what they saw.

'You're not lonely?' he asked.

'No, no, I don't have time; the twins keep me busy all day.'

'You get time off?'

'Not during the day and in the evening Sir Hugh and Lady Thorley get asked out a good deal, I believe.'

'But you get a free day?'

'Oh, yes—Wednesdays. There's a lot to see here, isn't there? I hope I stay long enough to see everything...'

He said diffidently, 'I'd be glad to show you round if you'd like that; I can always get an afternoon off. Next Wednesday perhaps?'

'Well, that would be nice...'

He heard the doubt in her voice. 'Sir Hugh knows me...' He grinned suddenly. 'I mean, I'll get him to introduce us properly if you like.'

Daisy laughed. 'No need. I would be glad of someone to show me round the Hague.'

'Good. I'll be free at half-past twelve. Do you think you could meet me? There's a brown café just across the street from the Bijenkorf—that's the big department store in the shopping street—you can't miss it.'

'Yes, of course. I must go and make sure that the children are all right.'

She bade him goodnight and went back up the stairs to the balcony where she paused to look down into the garden. It was somehow comforting to see the reflection of a lamp from his sitting-room window.

During the next few days she met some other English girls when she took the twins to the park. They were friendly, giving her useful tips—where to find the nearest hairdresser, the best shops to go to for humdrum things like toothpaste and tights, the cafés which served the cheapest food. They wanted to know if she had a boyfriend and gave her faintly pitying looks when she said that no, she hadn't. They considered that she was badly treated when it came to time off, too. 'You should have at least two evenings a week as well as a whole day; some of us get weekends...'

'I wouldn't know what to do with them,' said Daisy, 'and anyway I'm only here until Lady Thorley finds a governess.'

They smiled at her with faint patronage. A plain little thing, they told each other when she had left them.

Wednesday came with pleasing swiftness. Daisy had seen very little of Lady Thorley for there was a constant stream of visitors and she was out a good deal. True to her promise, she came to the play-room in good time for the children's breakfast this morning. 'I asked Corrie to take a tray to your room,' she told Daisy, 'and you go just as soon as you like. Will you be out late this evening?'

Daisy thought it unlikely; Philip Keynes hadn't mentioned any kind of evening entertainment. 'I don't think so, not this evening. Some of the girls I met in the park suggested that we might all go to a cinema on Wednesday evening but I expect I'll come back once the shops have shut.'

'Then I'll ask Mien to leave a tray for you in the kitchen. Have a pleasant day, Daisy; we shall miss you.'

Daisy gobbled her breakfast as she got ready to go out. She was a little excited; she had a week's pay in her purse and the prospect of a morning's window-shopping and then the unknown pleasures of the afternoon. She boarded a tram at the end of the road, thankful that it was a cool day so that the good suit didn't look out of place.

The shops were absorbing; she gazed into elegant boutique windows, shuddering at the prices, had coffee and spent the rest of her morning in de Bijenkorf, rather like a small Selfridges and more suited to her pocket. Not that she bought much but it was fun to go round the departments deciding what she would take home as presents, and at half-past twelve she crossed the road to the brown café and found Philip Keynes waiting for her.

She had felt a little shy of meeting him again but there had been no need; he was friendly, full of enthusiasm at the idea of showing her round the Hague, but it was a casual friendliness which quickly put her at her ease. He came from Bristol, he told her, and knew her home town quite well. Over coffee and *kaas broodjes* they talked about the West Country and its pleasures. 'I don't care much for cities,' he told her, 'but this is a good job and once I'm promoted I'll get a posting back home. What about you, Daisy? Do you want to travel before you settle down?'

'Not really. I'm glad I've had the chance to come here but when I get back home I'll find a local job.'

They didn't waste too much time over their lunch. He had the afternoon planned and kept to it. They visited the Ridderzaal and after that the Mauritshuis with its famous paintings. Daisy would have liked to have lingered there but she was urged on; the Kloosterkerk was a must, he told her; never mind that they could spend only a short time there—she would know where to go when next she went exploring and from there there was a glimpse of the eighteenth-century Kneuterdijk Palace. They stopped for tea then, this time in a café in Noordeinde, and it was as they emerged from it that Daisy came face to face with Dr Seymour. The pavements were crowded with people hurrying home from work, and since they were going in opposite directions it seemed unlikely that he had recognised her, but all the same she had been surprised at the sudden delight she had felt at the sight of him, instantly followed by the hope that she wouldn't meet him while he was in Holland. A good thing, she reflected, that she dined alone each evening; there would be no chance of meeting him if he came to see his sister...

She was recalled to her present whereabouts by her companion. 'I say, will it be all right if I put you on a tram? I've got to get to one of these official gatherings at the embassy. It's been a delightful afternoon; we must do it again.' He added anxiously, 'You hadn't any plans for this evening?'

'No, and I said I'd be back some time after tea, I've all kinds of odd jobs I want to do.' She saw the relief in his nice face. 'And you don't need to come with me to the tram; I know which one to catch.'

He wouldn't hear of that; they walked through the narrow streets together and he actually saw her on to a tram which would take her to the end of the road where the Thorleys were living. It was still early evening, but she had letters to write and her hair to wash and an hour or so just sitting with a book would be pleasant. She told herself this as she wished him goodbye, doubtful if he would repeat his invitation; she thought that she was probably rather a dull companion... All the same she had enjoyed the afternoon and she thanked him nicely for it and was surprised when he said, 'I meant it when I said we must do it again. A cinema, perhaps?'

'I'd like that.' She nipped on to the tram and was borne away at high speed down the Scheveningenscheweg, to get out at her stop and walk the short distance to the house.

The concierge admitted her with a muttered 'good evening' and Daisy, ignoring the lift, skipped up the stairs to the Thorleys' apartment and rang the bell. Corrie opened the door, bade her a cheerful hello and told her, in her peculiar English, that her dinner was ready whenever she liked to have it. Daisy thanked her and crossed the hall, to be stopped by Lady Thorley's voice from the half-open door of the drawing-room.

'Daisy?' she called. 'Come in here and tell us if you've had a nice day.'

The drawing-room was a grand room, rather over-furnished in a handsome way. Daisy crossed the parquet floor to the group of people sitting together at the far end by the open windows. She was halfway there when she saw that Dr Seymour was there too, standing leaning against the wall, a drink in his hand. There was a woman sitting there, a strikingly handsome woman in her early thirties and dressed in the kind of clothes Daisy, not given to envy, envied now.

'You know Dr Seymour already,' said Lady Thorley in her friendly way, 'and this is Mevrouw van Taal.'

Daisy said, 'How do you do?' and wished the doctor a good evening.

'You enjoyed your day?' Sir Hugh wanted to know. 'The Hague is a most interesting city. Of course you would have enjoyed it more if you had had a guide...'

Daisy glanced at the doctor. He was looking at her and smiling, a rather nasty little smile, she considered. So he had seen her after all. It was on the tip of her tongue to tell him that she had spent most of her day with Philip Keynes, but that might sound boastful and besides, he might not like that. She agreed quietly that it was indeed a most interesting city and it would take several days to explore it thoroughly.

There was a little silence and the *mevrouw* said in a sugary voice in faultless English, 'Well, I suppose if you have nothing better to do it passes the time.'

'Most agreeably,' said Daisy. 'Goodnight, Lady Thorley, Sir Hugh.' She smiled in the general direction of the doctor and Mevrouw van Taal and walked tidily out of the room, shutting the door gently behind her.

'I wish him joy of her,' she muttered as she went to her room.

The twins were asleep; she wondered what sort of a day their mother had had—she would hear in the morning, no doubt; in the meanwhile she would enjoy her dinner. She had been only a few minutes in the play-room when Corrie came in with a tray. Cold lettuce soup with a swirl of cream in its delectable greenness, chicken *à la* king, asparagus and game chips and a chocolate mousse to finish. Coffee too, brought by Corrie just as she had polished off the last of the mousse. Really, she thought, life couldn't be more pleasant. The unbidden thought that she was lonely crossed her mind, to be dismissed at once. It would have surprised her if she had heard the doctor, sitting at the dinner-table, waving away the chocolate mousse in favour of some cheese. 'Does Daisy not have her meals with you?' he asked idly.

'We almost always have lunch together—the two of us and the children. Of course Daisy could dine with us if she wished but she thought it would be better if she stayed in the play-room in case the children should wake.'

Lady Thorley sounded apologetic and then frowned when Mevrouw van Taal spoke. 'Well, one would hardly expect the nanny to dine, would one? Besides, it is likely that she has no suitable clothes. They have a garish taste in cheap clothes, these au pairs and nannies.'

Dr Seymour's face was inscrutable. He said mildly, 'One could hardly accuse Daisy of being garish.' He thought of the times he had seen her; mousy would be a more appropriate word, and that terrible plastic mackintosh...

The conversation became general after that and presently Mevrouw van Taal declared that she would really have to go home, smiling at the doctor as she said it. 'If someone would call a taxi?' she asked. 'Since my dear husband died I have not dared to drive the car.'

The doctor rose to his feet at once. 'Allow me to drive you back,' he said; his voice held nothing but social politeness. 'I have to go back to the hospital.'

An offer which Mevrouw van Taal accepted with rather too girlish pleasure.

Unaware that the doctor was spending the night at the apartment, Daisy slept peacefully; she still slept when he went down into the garden very early in the morning. There was a decidedly autumnal chill in the air but it was going to be another fine day. He strolled around and presently became aware that there was someone watching him—the occupier of the downstairs flat, leaning against the wall, behind the railings.

The doctor caught his eye, wished him good morning and was sure that he had seen him before—with Daisy yesterday afternoon. 'Are you not allowed to share the garden?' he enquired pleasantly. He held out a large well cared-for hand and thrust it through the railings. 'Valentine Seymour—Lady Thorley's brother—over here for a few days. I saw you yesterday with Daisy.'

Philip shook hands. 'Philip Keynes—I'm a clerk at the embassy. Yes, I showed Daisy something of the Hague. She's nanny to the children, but of course you know that.'

'Yes. She must have been glad of your company; it's hard to find one's way around a strange city.' The doctor leaned up against the railings. 'Have you been here long?'

'Almost a year; I'm hoping for promotion so that I can go back home! You're not at the embassy, are you?'

'No, no. I'm a paediatrician; I'm over here lecturing and seeing one or two patients that they've lined up for me. I live in London, but I have beds at Salisbury and at Southampton.' He glanced at his watch. 'I must go—I have to be in Utrecht soon after nine o'clock. I dare say we shall meet again.'

He went back upstairs to the balcony just as the twins, dressed and released to let off steam before breakfast, tore on to the balcony, screaming with delight at seeing him and followed at a more sedate pace by Daisy.

She stopped at the sight of him, uttered good morning in a small cool voice and added, 'They must have their breakfast.'

'So must I; shall I have it with you?'

He had spoken to the children and their shouts had drowned anything she might have wanted to say. Not that he would have taken any notice. He went into the play-room with them and found Corrie there, putting boiled eggs into egg-cups. She received the news that he was breakfasting with his nephew and niece with smiling nods, laid another place at the table and went away to get more eggs and toast. She came back presently with a plate of ham and cheese, a basket of rolls and croissants and a very large pot of coffee.

Daisy sat the children down, tied their bibs and poured cereal and milk into their bowls while the doctor leaned against a wall, watching, before pulling out her chair for her and seating himself opposite.

Daisy, pouring coffee and beakers of milk, had to admit to herself that he was good with children. They were, she suspected, a little in awe of him, and upon reflection she supposed that she was too but she found herself at ease and laughing with the children over the outrageous stories he was telling them. Daisy stopped abruptly at his quiet, 'You should laugh more often, Daisy, it turns you into a pretty girl.'

She went very pink. 'If that's meant to be a compliment I can do without it, Dr Seymour.'

'No, no, you mustn't misunderstand me; I was merely stating a fact.'

He spoke mildly and she felt a fool, her face reddening at his assured smile.

He passed his cup for more coffee. 'I had a talk with young Keynes—a sound young man—pity he's caged up behind those iron railings. Did you enjoy your afternoon with him, Daisy?'

'Yes, he knows where everything is...how did you know?'

'Well, I saw you, didn't I? Besides, I asked him this morning.'

Her small nose quivered with annoyance. Before she could speak he added, 'None of my business, is it? How do you like being a nanny?'

She said sedately, 'Very much, Doctor.' She got up to wipe the twins' small mouths and untie their bibs. 'And now if you will excuse us...?'

'Being put in my place, am I?' He got up too, tossed the children into the air, promised them sweets next time he came and made for the door, to turn and come back to where Daisy was standing, lift her firm little chin in his hand and stare down at her, his eyes, half hidden by their lids, studying her face.

'Kiss Daisy goodbye,' shrieked Katie, who, being female, was romantic even at four years old.

'Not this time,' said her uncle, and went unhurriedly from the room.

Daisy swallowed all the things she would have liked to utter; the twins were remarkably sharp for their age and they might repeat them to their mother and father. She urged the children along to the bathroom to wash teeth, faces and hands, vowing silently that if she saw Dr Seymour again she would run a mile, or at least go as quickly as possible in the opposite direction. Perhaps there would be no need to do that; hopefully he would be going back to England soon.

It was with relief that she heard Lady Thorley tell her that her brother had gone to Utrecht; she wouldn't have felt that relief, though, if Lady Thorley had added that he would be with them again that evening.

She spent the day on the beach with the children; there wouldn't be many more days in which to do that, she reflected. There was a distinct nip of autumn in the air now; October wasn't more than a few days away and already the beach kiosks and little seaside shops selling buckets and spades and postcards were putting up their shutters. Then it would be the park and, should they still be there, carefully planned hours to be spent in the play-room. She doubted, though, if she would be called upon to do that; long before then she would be back in Wilton, and if a governess had been found she would be looking for another job.

She took the children home in time for tea, and they had it with their mother in the play-room, and, much to Daisy's astonishment, Lady Thorley asked her if she would dine with them that evening. 'Just us,' she said. 'It will be nice to have a quiet evening. There's a reception tomorrow evening so we shall be out again—you've been very good and patient, Daisy, staying with the children; I'm sure I don't know what we should have done without you. Mrs Perry was telling me about Katwijk-aan-Zee—it's no distance away and she says it's so much nicer than Scheveningen—I thought I might drive you and the children there before it gets too chilly. I don't think I can spare the time to stay all day, but I could pick you up during the afternoon.'

Daisy agreed because she saw that Lady Thorley expected her to. One of the girls she had met in the park had told her it was a nice little seaside town and it would make a change.

She put the children to bed, read to them until they were sleepy and then changed into the blouse and skirt, did her face and hair with rather more care than usual and went on to the balcony to wait for the dinner-gong. It had been another fine day, now fading into a golden dusk, and the garden below looked inviting. She leaned on the balustrade and wondered if she had time to go down there, and decided against it just as Dr Seymour ranged himself alongside her.

He ignored her gasp of surprise. 'A delightful evening,' he observed pleasantly. 'There's a great deal of wide sky in Holland, isn't there?'

'Haven't you gone back to England yet?' asked Daisy, not bothering with the sky.

'Now that's the kind of encouraging remark I suppose I should have expected from you, Daisy.'

He turned his head to smile at her and she thought how very good-looking he was and so very large. 'You surprised me,' she told him.

'I'm relieved to hear that.' He smiled and this time it was kind. 'You're looking very smart this evening—Margaret tells me that you're dining with us.'

He had seen the beautifully washed and pressed blouse, certainly not new and decidedly out of date, and the skirt—a pretty colour which suited her and made, unless he was much mistaken, from what looked suspiciously like a curtain...

'Yes, Lady Thorley invited me, but perhaps now you're here—I mean, if she didn't know you were coming...'

'Oh, but she did—it will be an opportunity to talk about the twins; they seem very happy and they're fond of you.'

'They're very nice children.' She couldn't think of anything else to say, so that the faint sound of the gong came as a relief.

They went down together and he waited for her while she went to take a quick look at the twins, and, to her surprise, once they were downstairs sipping sherry before they went in to dinner, she forgot to feel shy, happy to find that Lady Thorley was wearing a blouse and skirt too—rather different from her own—oyster satin with a filmy black skirt and a jewelled belt. All the same Daisy felt at ease because she was wearing the right clothes.

They dined splendidly at a table covered with white damask, shining silver and gleaming glass; lobster bisque, guinea fowl with sautéd potatoes, artichokes and as-paragus followed by profiteroles with a great deal of cream, all nicely helped along with a white Bordeaux and then a sweet white wine she didn't much like to go with the pudding. There was brandy served with the coffee but she declined that. It seemed to her that nannies shouldn't do that; anyway, she wasn't sure that she would like brandy. She had maintained her part in the conversation very well and, since she was a good listener, Sir Hugh declared after she had said goodnight and gone upstairs that she had been a much more interesting table companion than Mevrouw van Taal. 'Nice manners too,' he observed. 'Do you agree, Val?'

'Oh, indeed, you have found yourselves a treasure—if a temporary one.'

'That reminds me,' said his sister, 'I was talking to Mrs Ross today—her husband's been posted to Brussels and her governess wants to go back to England. It seems she's a marvellous woman, splendid with small children and able to give lessons until they're old enough for school. Would it be a good idea if I found out a bit more about her? Personal recommendation is so much better than advertising.'

'That sounds promising,' Sir Hugh agreed. 'Make quick work of it, darling—I'll be here for another month at the outside; this paragon could take over when we get back home.' He paused. 'I'll be sorry to see Daisy go.'

'So shall I; she's so nice and gentle and kind. She should get a good job, though; I'll give her a splendid reference.'

To all of which conversation the doctor listened without saying a word; and, as for Daisy, blissfully unaware of what the future held in store for her, she put her head upon the pillow and went to sleep.

CHAPTER FOUR

DAISY woke with a pleasant feeling of excitement which, upon investigation, and to her surprise, was due to the fact that she would see the doctor again. She expected him to come and say hello to the twins—perhaps stay to breakfast—but there was no sign of him, nor did Lady Thorley mention him when she came to wish her children good morning after that meal. It wasn't until lunchtime, after she had taken the twins for a walk in the Scheveningse Bos, where there was plenty of open space in which they could tire themselves out, that Lady Thorley mentioned that her brother had gone back to England. 'He works too hard,' she complained. 'I tell him that he should marry, but he says he has no time for that. Such nonsense; one day he'll fall in love and then he'll find the time.'

As long as he didn't fall in love with someone like Mevrouw van Taal, reflected Daisy, and wondered why she disliked the idea so much; after all, she still wasn't sure if she liked him and he was surely old and wise enough to take care of himself.

The days unrolled themselves smoothly, each one rather like the last, until it was Wednesday again and Daisy, released from her duties, took the tram into the Hague. She had seen Philip Keynes on the previous evening and he had arranged to meet her at four o'clock for tea and then take her to the cinema. She was looking forward to it and now that she had some money in her pocket she would spend the morning looking for something for her mother and Pamela. Coffee first, she thought happily, as the tram deposited her at the stop nearest to the Bijenkorf.

She found a silver brooch for her mother and a silk scarf for her sister, both costing rather more than she could afford, so that her lunch was sparse, but in any case, she reminded herself, eating took up precious time and she planned to spend the afternoon, map in hand, getting some idea of the town. She lingered for some time along the Korte Vijverberg and the Lange Vijverberg, admiring the old houses with their variety of gabled roofs, and from there she walked to Lange Voorhout, pleasantly broad and tree-lined with its small palaces and embassies and luxurious Hotel des Indes. It must be pleasant working in such surroundings, she decided, thinking of Philip, even in the capacity of a clerk. She looked her fill at the patrician houses around her— a far cry from her own home; the thought of it made her feel homesick for a moment; it would be nice to see her mother and Pam again, but not just yet. Each week she was adding to her small nest-egg; a month, six weeks even, would allow her to put by more money than she had earned in months of work at the nursery school.

She strolled back to the café where she found Philip waiting for her. His pleasure at seeing her added to her enjoyment of her day and he was an easy person to talk to. They drank their tea and ate the rich cream-cakes so temptingly displayed and then made their way to the cinema.

It was a good film and there was time for a quick cup of coffee before they boarded the tram for home. Saying goodnight in the entrance to the flats, Daisy reflected that she hadn't enjoyed herself so much for a long time. Philip was the kind of man she would like to marry: easy to get on with, not given to sarcastic remarks and quite lacking in arrogance—unlike Dr Seymour, the sight of whose well-tailored appearance caused her instant annoyance.

She went indoors, spent ten minutes with the Thorleys describing her day and then went to her room, wondering if it was too late for her to get some supper. Tea had been delicious and the coffee after the cinema equally so but her insides were hollow.

She hadn't been in her room five minutes before Mien tapped on the door, bearing a tray. Soup in a pipkin, ham and a salad and coffee in a Thermos jug. A most satisfactory end to her day, she thought, gobbling her supper and then, after a last look at the twins, tumbling into her bed.

The weather changed, a mean wind blew and there was persistent rain. The twins reacted as might have been expected—tantrums, a refusal to do anything asked of them and a steady demand to go to the beach.

Lady Thorley finally gave way to their persistent small rages. 'Could you bear to go with them?' she asked Daisy. 'Perhaps if they went just once and got soaked they wouldn't want to go again—just for an hour or two?'

So Daisy buttoned them into their small mackintoshes, tied their hoods securely, stuffed their feet into wellies and then got into her plastic mac, tucking her hair under its unbecoming hood. They took a tram to the promenade and then, with buckets and spades, went down to the beach. Deserted, of course, and in a way Daisy liked it. The sea was rough and coldly grey and the wide sky was equally grey with the sandy shore below stretching away on either side as far as the eye could see. Lonely and magnificent and a bit frightening...

Daisy dispelled such a fanciful thought and got on to her knees the better to help build the sandcastle under Josh's shouted instructions.

They were to go back home for lunch, Lady Thorley had said, but there was time enough to build a dozen sandcastles. Daisy, fashioning a wall around the last of them, was startled by Katie's piercing shriek. The two children, shouting with delight, were hurtling up the beach towards Dr Seymour, making his leisurely way towards them. She got to her feet then, dusting the sand off her damp knees, looking just about as unglamorous as it was possible to look; the hood, never flattering, had slipped sideways so that a good deal of damp hair had escaped and her face was as damp as her knees.

She watched him coming towards her, a twin on either hand, wished him a good morning and stood quietly under his scrutiny, aware that she looked an absolute fright and hating him for it.

He smiled at her. 'Hello, Daisy, what marvellous sandcastles—I haven't made one for half a lifetime.' Unnoticing of the drizzle, he squatted down to inspect their work, fashioned a drawbridge, added an imposing tower, invited Daisy to admire them and got to his feet.

'Want a lift back?' he wanted to know. 'It's a bit early for lunch, but you'll all need a wipe down first, won't you?' His glance swept over Daisy and she lifted her chin. If he dared to smile... But he didn't. They went back up the beach to the promenade with the children happily hopping and skipping between them, making so much noise that there was no need to talk. A good thing, for she could think of nothing at all to say.

The Rolls was at the kerb and sitting in it was Mevrouw van Taal.

'You know each other, don't you?' observed the doctor easily as he stuffed the children into the back of the car. 'Hop in between them, Daisy.'

Mevrouw turned an elegant shoulder to look at them. 'What a very strange way in which to spend the morning,' she said acidly, 'but of course I suppose it doesn't matter to you when you do not need to bother with your appearance.'

Daisy thought of several things to say and uttered none of them; it was the twins who yelled rudely at her, protesting that the beach in the rain was the nicest thing they knew of, a sentiment echoed by their uncle, who had got into the car, taken a quick look at Daisy's outraged face and smoothly taken the conversation into his own hands, so that the twins, hushed by Daisy, subsided, allowing him to carry on a desultory exchange of remarks with Mevrouw van Taal. When they arrived at the house she whisked them upstairs to be washed and tidied for their lunch, and they were so pleased with the idea of their uncle having lunch with them that they forgot all about Mevrouw van Taal. But, when they were led into the dining-room, faced with the sight of that lady sitting by their uncle, sipping sherry, their small faces puckered into scowls.

'Why——?' began Josh, and was hushed by Daisy.

'Tell Mummy about the castles we built this morning,' she urged.

He went obediently but his lower lip was thrust out in an ominous manner. It was Katie who spoke in her shrill voice. 'I thought Uncle Val was having lunch with us, not with her,' she observed.

'Well, we are all having lunch together,' observed Daisy. 'Do tell Daddy about that crab you found.' She caught the doctor's eye and saw that he was laughing silently. Let him, she thought savagely, and looked away from his mocking glance.

Mien came to the door then to announce that lunch was ready, which was a good thing—the children had a look on their faces which boded no good. She prayed silently that they would behave themselves at table.

The prayer wasn't answered; it was unfortunate that Mevrouw van Taal was seated opposite them, and Daisy, sitting between them, knew without looking that they had fixed their large blue eyes upon her and at any moment would say something outrageous...

'Which reminds me,' said Dr Seymour apropos of nothing at all, 'I have something for you two—you may have it after lunch if your mother says you may, on condition that you're extra-good.'

Daisy let out a relieved breath and then drew it in again sharply when the doctor winked at her from a bland face. Really, the man was simply impossible. She busied herself attending to the children and was thankful that they were behaving like small angels. Their father paused in the middle of a sentence to ask if they were sickening for something. 'You must have performed a

miracle on them, Daisy,' he said kindly. 'Let us hope . . .'
he caught his wife's eye ' . . . that it lasts,' he ended tamely.
He had forgotten for the moment that Daisy hadn't been
told that the new governess would be taking over very
shortly—something which would have to be broken to
the children at the proper time, which wasn't now.

Mevrouw van Taal could be charming in the right
company. Daisy had to admire her—she had good looks,
the right clothes and a helpless-little-girl manner which
Daisy felt simply certain would appeal to any man. She
was an amusing talker too; Daisy allowed her rather high-
pitched voice to go over her head while she thought about
the doctor. Was he here for a long stay, she wondered,
or a lightning visit? She frowned; it was no concern of
hers anyway, only it would be nice to know . . .

The twins were allowed down from the table once the
pudding had been eaten; they kissed their parents, stared
stonily at Mevrouw van Taal as they muttered what Daisy
hoped was a polite goodbye.

'Run along with Daisy, darlings,' begged their mother.
'We'll have coffee in the drawing-room, shall we?' she
said to the others.

Dr Seymour got up to open the door and bent his
massive person to whisper to Josh, 'Wait in the hall; I'll
be out in a moment.'

He went back into the room, leaving the door half-
open so that Mevrouw van Taal's voice was very audible
to Daisy, waiting at the foot of the stairs with the twins.

'Charming children,' she declared, 'and so well behaved. That girl—their nanny—is the quiet sort, isn't
she? Plain with it too.' She gave a tinkle of laughter. 'Let
us hope she is as quiet and kind when she is alone with

the children...' Daisy, rigid with rage, heard the Thorleys protest as the woman went on, 'Oh, I didn't mean to upset you, I'm sure she is a very good young woman, but one does hear such tales.'

'Not about Daisy.' It was the doctor, speaking in such a cold voice that Daisy shivered. 'I'm sure you meant no harm, Rena, but it is perhaps a little unwise to give an opinion of someone of whom you know nothing, is it not?'

He came into the hall a moment later, shutting the door behind him.

'I'm sorry if you heard that; I'm sure Mevrouw van Taal meant nothing personal.'

'I don't care what she means,' said Daisy in a stony voice. 'Pray don't bother to make excuses for her. If you would be good enough to give the children their present I can take them upstairs so that I may be discussed at your ease.'

'Spitfire,' said Dr Seymour mildly and added, 'You have very lovely eyes.'

'Ah—you forget, a plain face...'

'We'll discuss that some time.' He smiled very kindly at her and she felt tears crowding her throat, which made her crosser than ever.

'There's a small box on the hall table,' he told the children. 'Will you fetch it, Josh?'

It was actually quite a big box; he opened it and took out two smaller boxes and gave them to the children. 'Not to be opened until you're lying on your beds.' He bent down and kissed their excited faces and then, in an afterthought, kissed Daisy too.

'I'm going away directly,' he told her. 'You'll be glad, won't you?'

'Yes,' said Daisy, not meaning it. She urged the twins upstairs and didn't look back.

The boxes contained musical boxes, the sort which, when wound, displayed a group of dancing figures on their lids. The twins were enchanted with them and quite forgot to be difficult about taking their afternoon nap, so that Daisy found herself with nothing to do until they woke again. It was still raining and she turned her back on the dismal weather, got out her pen and writing pad and began a letter to her mother, anxious to occupy her thoughts with something other than dwelling on the kiss Dr Seymour had given her. It was exactly the same kind of kiss as those he had bestowed upon his small relations, and she hoped that it hadn't been bestowed in pity; she hoped too, with quite unnecessary fervour, that he would be gone by the time she went downstairs with the children again.

Fate always answered the wrong prayers; there was no sign of him when the children went down to have tea with their mother; moreover he was already on his way back to England, Lady Thorley told her. 'He will be back, though, for a few days shortly,' she continued, 'some meeting or other in Leiden.'

All memories of the summer were being washed away by a persistent fine rain, and the twins' high spirits, because they were largely confined to indoors, were rapidly turning to fits of sulks and displays of childish rage. Daisy took them out each day despite the wind and rain and the three of them, swathed in mackintoshes and hoods and sensible shoes, went to the park, empty of people now, where they ran races and then went home, sopping-wet and tired, but by the afternoon their energy was firmly restored, and Daisy was glad when it was bedtime and she could tuck them up. Of course, they were reluctant to sleep and she read to them until she was hoarse...

It rained on her day off too, which was a pity, for Philip had borrowed a friend's car and had promised to drive her to Apeldoorn then down to Arnhem through the Hoge Veluwe National Park and then back to the Hague. All the same they went, making light of the weather, and Philip, who prided himself on the knowledge he had of the Dutch countryside, took pains to point out everything interesting in sight. Even in the rain Apeldoorn was pleasant; they had their soup and a roll in a small café on the edge of the town and then set off for Arnhem. The road ran through wooded country and stretches of heath, the villages were small and infrequent and here and there they caught glimpses of large villas half-hidden by trees, and when they reached Arnhem he took her round the open-air museum where Holland's way of life was portrayed by farms, windmills and houses from a bygone age. Despite the rain, Daisy would have lingered for hours but it was quite some distance back to the Hague and they simply had to have tea...

Back at the house they parted like old friends. 'I'll get the car next week,' Philip promised, 'and we'll go north to Alkmaar and Leeuwarden. You're not going back home yet, are you?'

'No, I don't think so yet; I heard Sir Hugh saying that he expected to be here for another month or even longer.'

'Good. I'll see you next week.' She rang the bell and watched him get into the car to drive it back to his friend's flat. It had been a lovely day and Philip was an undemanding companion, always ready to agree with her suggestions. He would make a nice brother, she thought, as Mien opened the door and she went inside.

Mien took her wet things and nodded her head upstairs where small cross voices could be heard. 'It is good that you are back. Lady Thorley is weary. The children...' She raised her hands and rolled her eyes up to the ceiling.

Daisy sped upstairs and found Lady Thorley attempting to get the twins quiet. They were bellowing and screaming and quite out of hand but they paused long enough to shout at Daisy.

'If you're quiet,' said Daisy, 'I'll tell you where I've been today, so say goodnight to Mummy and lie down, there's dears.'

Lady Thorley gave her a thankful look, kissed them and went to the door. 'I'll tell Mien to send you up a tray in half an hour, Daisy.' She asked belatedly, 'You had a nice day?'

'Delightful, thank you, better than yours.'

Lady Thorley made a face. 'They need a dragon to look after them. I'll say goodnight, and thank you, Daisy.'

Getting ready for bed a few hours later, Daisy prayed once more, this time for fine weather; much more of the twins' naughtiness would make even her stout heart quail; at least out of doors they tired themselves out.

This time her prayers were answered; the really heavy rain ceased and although the wind was chilly and the sky overcast at least they could get out. Three days passed in comparative peace and on the fourth morning, just as they had finished their breakfast, Dr Seymour walked into the play-room.

The twins were delighted to see him and, although she wouldn't admit it to herself, Daisy was too. Disentangling himself from the twins' embrace, he addressed himself to her. 'I'll keep an eye on these two—Margaret would like you to go down to the sitting-room; she wants to talk to you.'

There had been some talk of buying warmer clothes for the children; Daisy, nipping smartly along the passage, rehearsed in her head the various garments which would be necessary.

Lady Thorley was at the breakfast table and Sir Hugh was still there too. Daisy, her mind engaged in the choice of Chilprufe as against Ladybird vests, wished them both good morning and, when bidden to sit, sat.

'We wanted to talk to you,' began Lady Thorley, and looked at her husband, who coughed and said,

'Er—well, it's like this, Daisy...' and coughed again. 'You know, of course, that we engaged you on a temporary basis; indeed, we had intended that you should stay with us until we returned to England in a few weeks' time. However, a colleague of mine is being posted and the governess he employs for his children does not wish to stay with them but wants to return to England. We thought at first that she might take over from you when we go back there but it would make it much easier for everyone concerned if she were to come straight to us here. We think that if she were to join us here in two days' time you might spend a day with her—show her the ropes—and return to England on the following day. We will, of course, arrange your journey and, needless to say, a very good reference.'

Daisy said in a polite voice, 'That seems a very sensible arrangement, Sir Hugh. I'm glad you've found a governess; it's so much better to have someone recommended, isn't it?'

She heard herself uttering the words she felt sure her companions wished to hear while inwardly she fought unhappy surprise. She had felt secure at least for another month, which had been silly of her, and she was quite unprepared for such a sudden decision on the part of the Thorleys. Something of her thoughts must have shown on her face for Lady Thorley said quickly, 'You do understand that we have never been less than absolutely satisfied with you, Daisy. You've been splendid with the twins; I don't know how I would have managed without you . . .'

'I've enjoyed looking after them, Lady Thorley. If there's nothing else I'll go and get the children ready for their walk.' Daisy got up. 'I expect you know that Dr Seymour is with the twins?'

'Yes. He's due at the hospital this afternoon; he'll be going back home some time this evening.' Lady Thorley smiled at Daisy. 'Run along, then; if I don't see you at lunch, I'll be here in good time for the twins' tea.'

The doctor was sitting on the table, the breakfast things pushed to one side, and the children were beside him; the three heads were close together but they looked up as she went in.

'If you go to the hall,' said the doctor, 'you might find something in the umbrella stand by the door; if you do, take it to your father and mother and ask if you may have it.'

When they had scampered off he got off the table and went to stand before her. 'Surprised?' he asked.

'You knew? That I'm going back to England?'

'Yes. Hugh asked me what I thought about it some time ago when he first heard of this governess. I think it's a splendid idea; they need a female sergeant major to look after them. You're a splendid nanny, I should suppose, but you're too kind and forgiving, my dear; they'll be twisting you round their thumbs in a few months.'

'That's an unkind remark to make,' said Daisy coldly, 'but I suppose only to be expected of you. I know your opinion of me is low...' She added with a snap, 'Not that I care about that.' She drew a sustaining breath. 'I shall be sorry to leave the twins but nothing will give me greater pleasure than the thought that I need never see you again.' She went to the door. 'Now if you will excuse me, Dr Seymour, I will go to the children.' Her hand on the doorknob, she turned to look at him over her shoulder. 'I do hope Mevrouw van Taal manages to catch you; you deserve her.'

She didn't exactly sweep out of the room—she was too small for that—but she managed a dignified exit.

The doctor stood there where she had left him, the outrage on his face slowly giving way to a wide grin.

Daisy buttoned the children into their outdoor things and took them for their walk. She would have liked time to sit down and think about the turn of events; she had known that the job was temporary but she had expected to have a longer warning of its finish so that she could have made plans about getting work when she got home. Now there would be no time to do that and although she had saved up almost all of her wages it might be weeks before she found another job. There was no time to worry about that now, though; the twins, intent on reaching the park to see if any of their small friends were also there, hurried her along, both talking at once, leaving her no time at all for her own thoughts. Which was just as well.

Nothing was to be said to the children until the new governess arrived; Daisy, carrying on with their usual routine during the next two days, wondered if they would like her. Dr Seymour had described her as a sergeant major... She wished she could stop thinking about him; he had gone as swiftly as he had come, and presumably he was back in England. She reminded herself that she had no wish to see him ever again and, once the children were in their beds, began to get her clothes ready to pack.

The sergeant major arrived after breakfast as Daisy was arranging painting books and paints on the playroom table; the dull morning had made it easy to persuade the twins that a walk later in the day would be a better idea so that when their mother and the new governess came into the room they were engaged in quarrelling amicably together as to who should have the bigger paintbox.

Daisy put a jar of water in the centre of the table out of harm's way, smiled at Lady Thorley and said good morning to her companion. The woman was a good deal older than herself, tall and thin and good-looking, but she looked kind and when Lady Thorley said, 'This is

Amy Thompson, Daisy,' she held out her hand and gave Daisy a firm handshake.

The children had come to stand by Daisy, eyeing the stranger with suspicion; it was their mother who said coaxingly, 'Come and say hello to Miss Thompson; she's going to spend the day with us...'

'Why?' asked Josh and then, urged by Daisy, offered a small hand.

'Well,' began his mother, 'Miss Thompson is going to live with us and be your governess; you're going to have lessons at home, which will be much more fun than going to school...'

Katie shook hands too, eyeing the newcomer. 'We'd rather keep Daisy,' she observed.

Josh's bottom lip was thrust forward in an ominous manner and Daisy said quickly, 'The thing is, my dears, I do have to go home and live with my mother and sister...'

Katie burst into tears and Josh flung himself on to the floor, where he lay kicking and shouting. Daisy got down beside him. 'Look, Josh, we'll still see each other; I live very close to your home, you know—perhaps Miss Thompson will invite me to tea sometimes and allow you both to come and see Razor.'

He opened an eye. 'Promise?'

Daisy glanced at Miss Thompson who nodded and smiled. 'Promise,' said Daisy, 'and now if you will get up and Katie will stop crying we can have some fun showing Miss Thompson where everything is and what you wear when you go out and just how you like your eggs boiled. She will really depend on you both for a little while, just as I had to when I first came to look after you.'

It took time to coax the children to calm down, something they did unwillingly, but Miss Thompson was a veteran at the job; by lunchtime they were on good terms with her, with only the occasional suspicious look. She went away at teatime with the assurance that she would return the following morning.

With Josh and Katie in bed, Daisy packed, washed her hair, checked the contents of her handbag and went downstairs to dine with the Thorleys. Sir Hugh gave her her ticket. 'One of the drivers will take you to Schiphol,' he told her. 'We thought if you took the late morning flight—Miss Thompson will be here at ten o'clock, and it might be easier if you go shortly afterwards, in case the children...'

He paused, and Daisy said, 'Yes, of course, I quite understand.'

'You'll go home by train? You'll find travelling expenses in that envelope—you'll have to go up to London from Gatwick unless you can get a bus to Basingstoke.'

'Either way will be easy,' said Daisy; she sounded as though she knew what she was talking about although she had only the vaguest idea about the train service to Salisbury from London; but there were bound to be several and she would be at Gatwick by one o'clock at the latest.

Sir Hugh said thankfully, 'Oh, good, it should be quite simple. Do telephone your mother if you wish to...'

She decided against that; she wasn't sure what time she would get home and her mother would worry. They went in to dinner and she joined in the conversation in her quiet way, all the while not quite believing that in twenty-four hours' time she would be home again and out of a job once more.

She hated leaving the twins; she was quite sure that Miss Thompson would be kind as well as seeing to their education, but all the same it was a wrench and all the harder since she had to keep a cheerful face on things when she said goodbye. It was a wet morning; the last she saw of them was two small faces pressed against the play-room windows. She waved until the car turned into the street, and since the driver was disinclined for conversation she spent the journey to the airport musing over a choice of jobs. Another nanny's post perhaps? Or a mother's help? Failing those, how about working in a shop? But wouldn't she have to know something about selling things? How did one start? she wondered. She was still wondering when they reached Schiphol and the driver fetched her case from the boot and carried it to the desk for her. She thanked him, gave him a tip and joined the queue of passengers being processed towards their various flights.

The flight was uneventful; she collected her case from the carousel, went through Customs and to the entrance, borne along on a stream of people intent on getting home as quickly as possible. There were taxis there and, some distance away, a bus. She picked up her case, to have it taken from her at the same time as Dr Seymour said quietly. 'The car's over here.'

She turned round and gaped up at him. 'That's my case,' she told him sharply. 'And I'm not going by car; there's a bus...' She drew breath. 'How did you get here, and why?'

'How you do chatter.' He took her arm. 'I'm on my way back to Salisbury. Margaret rang me this morning and mentioned that you would be on this flight; it seemed only good sense to collect you on my way.'

They had reached the car and he had opened the door and stuffed her inside and put her case in the boot; now he got in beside her. She was still thinking of something to say as, with the minimum of fuss, he drove away from the airport.

'Had a good trip?' he asked casually.

'Yes. Thank you.' She had remembered that she had never wanted to see him again and she sounded waspish.

'Still peeved?'

Hateful man. 'I don't know what you mean, and please don't feel that you have to—to entertain me with conversation; I have no wish to come with you. Probably you mean it kindly but I thought I had made it clear that I didn't want to see you again...'

They were away from the airport and the big car surged silently forward.

'Yes, yes, I know that, and if you're bent on keeping to your rigid principles I won't say another word; you can sit there and pretend I'm not here.'

And he didn't. They went down the M3 at a spanking pace, slowed to go through Salisbury and ten minutes later slowed again as they reached Wilton. He stopped outside her home, got out, opened her door, fetched her case and banged the knocker on the door.

'Thank you for the lift,' said Daisy. 'Would you like a cup of coffee or—or something?' She looked as far as his tie and then gave him a quick glance. He was looking down at her, an eyebrow raised to mock her.

'My dear Daisy, is this an olive-branch?' He turned to the door as it opened and Mrs Pelham gave a small shriek of delight.

'Daisy, darling—how lovely.'

She looked enquiringly at the doctor and Daisy said, 'Hello, Mother. This is Dr Seymour, who kindly brought me home...'

'That's twice,' said her mother, and smiled at him. 'Come in and have a cup of tea.'

'I should have liked that, Mrs Pelham, but I've an appointment.'

Mrs Pelham nodded sympathetically. 'Well, of course, you doctors don't have much time to spare, do you?'

He had nice manners; his goodbyes weren't to be faulted but the eyes he rested upon Daisy were as cold and hard as granite.

They waited until the Rolls had reached the end of the street before they went indoors.

'Such a lovely surprise,' said her mother. 'I thought you wouldn't be home for another few weeks, dear.'

'Well, so did I, Mother, but there was a governess who'd been with friends of the Thorleys and she's taken over the twins.'

'Well, I'll put on the kettle and you shall tell me all about it. Pam will be home soon; she will be pleased.'

Mrs Pelham led the way into the kitchen. 'That nice doctor driving you back like that. Did he meet you at the airport?'

'He was on his way to Salisbury and the Thorleys did tell him which flight I'd be on.'

'Now that is what I call kind; you must have had a delightful journey together.'

Daisy took off her jacket. 'Oh, yes, we did, indeed we did.' She uttered the lie so heartily that she almost believed it herself.

CHAPTER FIVE

PAMELA came home when Daisy was halfway through the account of her stay in Holland, so she would have to begin all over again, but before she had a chance to start her sister said, 'Do tell; this Philip you wrote about, is he nice? Will you see him again?'

'Perhaps, if he comes home on leave and he hasn't forgotten me. He had planned to take me to the north of Holland but I've come home instead—I only had a few minutes in which to say goodbye.'

Her mother said, 'There, I knew you'd meet someone nice.'

'He was just a friend, Mother; I think he felt lonely and he enjoyed showing me round the Hague.'

Her mother looked disappointed. 'Yes, well, dear... did you meet anyone else while you were there?'

Daisy refilled the teapot from the kettle. 'Friends of the Thorleys—there are a lot of English people living there—and Dr Seymour; he's abroad a great deal and he came to see them while I was there.'

'He didn't bring you all the way home?'

'No, I told you, he was on his way from London to Salisbury and Lady Thorley had told him I would be coming back on the late morning flight.'

'So kind,' commented her mother. 'It's lovely to have you home, Daisy.' She glanced at Pamela. 'We've managed quite well, I think.'

'I knew you would. I've almost all of my wages; I'll go to the bank tomorrow and pay them in.'

'Yes, dear. Now I'm going to get us a nice supper while you unpack.'

It was much later, after Pam had gone to bed and her mother was sitting contentedly knitting, that Daisy took a look at the housekeeping purse and then leafed through the chequebook. Even in those few weeks while she had been away the money seemed to have melted away alarmingly; she would have to start looking for a job as soon as possible.

She spent a couple of days at home, sorting out the small problems her mother had, paying one or two bills which had been overlooked, catching up with the local news and tidying the garden. After the weekend, she promised herself, she would start looking for a job.

There was nothing in the local paper on Saturday so she cycled into Salisbury on Monday morning, bought all the magazines which advertised work and visited two agencies. Neither of them had anything for her; there was, it seemed, no demand for mother's helps, nannies or unqualified kindergarten teachers. 'Now if you had simple typing and shorthand,' suggested the brisk lady at the second agency Daisy went to, 'I could offer you several good jobs. I suppose you haven't had any experience in a shop? There's a good opening for an experienced sales girl in a fancy goods shop.'

Daisy shook her head; she wasn't sure what fancy goods were anyway, and the lady gave her a scornful look. 'Well, dear, all I can suggest is that you take a course in something and then try again—there's always domestic work or work for early morning office cleaners...'

It might even come to that, thought Daisy. How fortunate it was that there was a little money in the bank, enough to keep them all for several weeks, although the uneasy thought that she would have to order coal for the winter very soon haunted her... There was no point in getting pessimistic, she told herself; after all, she had only just started to look for work.

She spent the week applying for various jobs she found in the magazines but they were few and none of the advertisers bothered to answer her applications. So she sat with Razor on her lap, writing an advert to put in the local paper, and had to admit that her skills were too limited to attract more than the casual eye. All the same, she sent it off and went along to the job centre.

There wasn't anything there, either; it seemed that she was unemployed. But things could have been worse; the local bakery needed part-time help—Friday mornings and Saturday afternoons for two weeks only. It was quite hard work and she didn't get on very well with the till but the money was a godsend, little though it was. She received her wages for the last time and started to clear up in the shop before she went home. The manageress was totalling the day's takings and was disposed to be friendly.

'Well, you've not done too badly, love,' she observed, 'though I can see it's not quite your cup of tea; still, anything's better than having no work, isn't it?'

Daisy, wiping down the counter, agreed. 'I've liked working here. I dare say something will turn up soon.'

However, it didn't, and September was nudging its way into October. Daisy ordered the coal; paying for it left a hole in the bank account, a hole which would have to be filled. She cycled to Salisbury again and tried the two agencies once more; the first one had nothing at all, the second offered her work as a mother's help in a family of six children living on a farm at Old Sarum; she would have to live in and the wages were low. Daisy said that she would think about it and despite her lack of money went and had a cup of coffee. If only something would happen, she reflected as she drank it.

It was as well that she was unaware that Dr Seymour was drinking coffee too—in her mother's kitchen. He had called, he told Mrs Pelham, on the spur of the moment. 'I know my sister will want to know if Daisy has found a good job and I shall be seeing her shortly.'

Mrs Pelham gave him a second cup of coffee and offered biscuits. 'Daisy's gone to Salisbury to see those two agencies again; there's nothing, you know, and you have no idea how difficult it is to find work, and the dear child isn't trained for anything—you see, my husband died and there was such a lot to see to and I'm not very businesslike and then we found that there wasn't enough money so she took that job with Mrs Gower-Jones—it was just enough with my pension.'

'So Daisy has no work yet?'

'Well, she helped out at the local bakery for two weeks, just for two half-days a week.' Mrs Pelham paused. 'I really don't know why I'm bothering you with all this...'

'Perhaps I can be of help. I happen to know that the hospital is short of ward orderlies—not domestics but they help with all the small tasks so that the nurses have more time for their own work.' And since Mrs Pelham was looking bewildered he explained, 'Helping with the meals, tidying beds, arranging flowers and so on. I believe that the hours are reasonable and the pay is adequate; at least it might tide her over until she finds something more to her taste.'

'She wouldn't need any training?' asked Mrs Pelham eagerly.

He said gently, 'No, just common sense and kindness, and she has both.'

'I'll tell her the moment she gets in...'

'Why not? But I think it might be a good idea if you don't mention that I've been to see you or that I've told you of the job; I think Daisy might resent anything which smacks of charity and it might seem like that to her. Could you not say that you've heard of work at the hospital from some friend or acquaintance?'

'Well, yes, I can do that; we know a great many people in the town—I could have heard about it from a dozen people. And I see what you mean about not telling Daisy that you called and told me about it; she is a dear girl but very independent.'

They had another cup of coffee together and parted on the best of terms and Mrs Pelham sat down and rehearsed what she would say to Daisy when she got home, pausing to regret that the doctor seemed to have no interest in Daisy; his voice had been impersonal when he had talked of her, and why should it have been otherwise? Daisy was no beauty and she had a way of saying exactly what she thought which could be disconcerting; perhaps she had annoyed him in some way, in which case it was kind of him to put himself to the trouble of finding her a job and in all probability he was only doing what his sister had asked him to do.

Daisy, despondent at her lack of success, listened eagerly to her mother's news when she returned home. 'I met Mrs Grenville—remember her, dear? She lives somewhere in Salisbury. She was at the market and we got chatting. She told me that they need these orderlies at the hospital; they're going to advertise but if you went along you might stand a chance before it gets into the paper.'

'I'll go in the morning; I can at least apply if there really are vacancies.'

It wasn't until she woke up in the middle of the night that she remembered Dr Seymour worked at the hospital. Unfortunate, she thought sleepily, but that was a small hindrance compared with the possibility of a secure job.

She telephoned the hospital the next morning and was told that yes, applicants were to be interviewed for several vacancies for ward orderlies and if she cared to present herself at two o'clock that day, bringing with her two references, she would be seen some time during the afternoon.

It was rather daunting to find that she was one of many and one of the last to be interviewed.

She hadn't much chance of getting a job, she reflected, answering the questions the severe woman behind the desk was asking her, unaware that the severe lady had been discreetly told that, should a Miss Daisy Pelham present herself for an interview, Dr Seymour would vouch for her personally. Thoroughly reliable, hardworking and trustworthy, he had said, previously employed by his sister and leaving only because the children had grown too old for a nanny.

The severe lady did not mention this for the simple reason that she had been told not to; she merely told Daisy that she would be notified if she was successful.

'I'm not very hopeful,' said Daisy as she had supper with her mother and sister that evening. 'There were dozens of us there and most of them looked frightfully efficient.'

'We'll have to wait and see,' sighed her mother placidly.

They didn't have to wait long; there was a letter the next morning confirming her appointment as a ward orderly, starting on the following Monday. She was to report for work at half-past eight each morning except for Saturdays and Sundays, but she would be expected to work one weekend in four. The wages were adequate; there would be no money to spare but they would be solvent. They had a rather excited breakfast and Pamela said, 'I'm glad you've got a job, Daisy, but you're not to stay a ward orderly a day longer than you must—if something better turns up... Will the work be rather beastly? Cleaning up after patients and fetching and carrying for the nurses?'

'It will be interesting,' said Daisy stoutly.

When she presented herself in a wrap-around pink overall on Monday morning she really found it more than interesting—thoroughly bewildering. She was to work on Women's Medical with another orderly, a woman in her thirties, who, Daisy quickly discovered, did her work with a kind of dogged thoroughness, disregarding the occupants of the beds—indeed, they might as well have been empty for all the notice she took of them. Daisy, friendly by nature, smiled at the patients, moved their glasses of water where they could reach them, picked up their knitting dropped on the floor and unreachable, and exchanged magazines and papers.

'You'll never get your work done while you waste your time with them,' observed Mrs Brett sourly. 'Just you collect up them empty cups and take them out to the kitchen. The trolley's on the landing.'

So Daisy collected cups, wiped locker-tops, collected water jugs and ran errands for Sister, who, beyond asking her her name and telling her to do whatever Mrs Brett told her to do, had had nothing more to say to her. Mrs Brett, relishing her superiority, told her to do a great deal: carry round the trays at lunchtime, help frail elderlies to the loo, change sheets in the beds of those who had had unfortunate accidents and hurry with bowls to those who felt sick. It was all very muddled and Daisy wasn't sure if she was going to like it; Mrs Brett was far too bossy and the nurses were too busy to see it...

She was sent to the canteen for her lunch at half-past twelve and was much more cheered to find several girls of her own age at the table, orderlies like herself and prepared to be friendly, and when she told them where she was working a comfortably plump girl with a pleasant country accent observed kindly that it was hard luck having to work with Mrs Brett, who had been at the hospital for a long time and behaved as though she ran the place. 'A pity that once you get a ward you stay on it, though you might be lucky and get moved.'

Daisy went back for the afternoon's work feeling more cheerful; it was, after all, her first day and probably Mrs

Brett would be nicer when they got to know each other. Mrs Brett, however, wasn't disposed to be friendly; indeed if anything she became more sharp-tongued as the afternoon wore on. Daisy, her day's work done, went home and presented a cheerful face to her mother and sister; the work was interesting, she was sure she was going to like it, and to her mother's enquiry as to whether she had met any of the doctors on the ward she said no, not yet, not wishing to disappoint her parent with the fact that the doctors, even the young housemen, didn't so much as cast a glance in her direction and weren't likely to either; an orderly was a domestic after all.

By the end of the week she had come to the conclusion that Mrs Brett, for all her bossiness, wasn't organised; there was a great deal of time wasted over their various jobs and far too much to-ing and fro-ing. Besides, she didn't much like the way Mrs Brett tossed knives, spoons and forks on to the patients' beds ready for their meals, so that some of the less agile patients had to wait until someone bringing their lunch- or tea-tray scooped them up and handed them over. Daisy knew better than to say anything and, uncaring of Mrs Brett's cross voice, nipped around arranging things within reach, and tidily too, and when Mrs Brett wasn't looking cutting up food and filling water glasses. She got the sharp edge of her colleague's tongue several times a day but she ignored that. One day, she promised herself, she would tell Mrs Brett just what she thought of her. It was a great pity that she was allowed to do more or less what she liked on the ward but to Sister she presented an appearance of hard-working efficiency, ready with the tea-tray when that lady sat down in her office to do the paperwork and running errands for the nurses. The patients didn't like her; indeed, some of the elderlies who depended on a helping hand were a little afraid of her.

Daisy, going home at the end of the first week with her pay packet in her pocket, decided that even if she didn't much like being an orderly the job provided her family's bread and butter and gave her the chance to help some of the patients.

'Have you seen anything of Dr Seymour?' her mother asked that evening.

'Him?' Daisy had washed her hair and was winding an elaborate turban around her head. 'No, but he works in London, as well you know. Probably he only comes to Salisbury when he's needed.'

'A pity, but at least you'll see something of the Thorleys when they come back, won't you?'

'I expect so. I promised the children I'd go and see them.'

She had been happy with Josh and Katie, she reflected and, despite the fact that she never wanted to see Dr Seymour again, she had been unable to forget him. He would have forgotten her already, of course.

Halfway through the next week she met him face to face on her way back from her lunch; there was no one else in sight and she debated whether to stop and speak to him—a wasted exercise for he gave her a wintry smile, nodded briefly and walked past her. She stood, watching him go out of sight; she still wasn't sure just how important he was; if the young housemen ignored the domestic staff, she supposed that the more senior medical staff were hardly aware of any but the senior nursing staff. All the same, he could have said something—hello would have done...

Gobbling bread and butter and drinking strong tea with some of the other orderlies during her brief tea break, she suddenly realised that they were talking about him.

'Marvellous with the kids,' said a voice, 'a pity we don't see more of him; comes twice a week for his out-patients and ward-rounds; ever so polite too—says good morning as affable as you like, more than some I know...'

There was general laughter. 'Well, what do you expect? No one's going to look twice at the likes of us. He's different, though—a real gent.'

'Married, is 'e?' asked one of the girls.

'Well, I don't know him well enough to ask...' There was a good deal of good-natured laughter as they got up to go back to their wards.

It must be that he didn't like her, reflected Daisy, hurrying along corridors and up stairs; if he had said good morning to the other girls, why couldn't he have done the same to her? She had quite overlooked the fact that she told him in no uncertain terms that she had no wish to see him again.

That afternoon, when she was cycling home after work, the Rolls whispered past her. The doctor was looking straight ahead and there was a good deal of traffic on the road; he wouldn't have seen her. All the same, she wished most unreasonably that he had at least lifted a hand in salute.

When she got home her mother said in a pleased voice, 'Lady Thorley phoned, love. They came back today and the children want to see you. I told her you were only free at the weekends—she said she'd ring again.' She glanced at Daisy's face. 'You've had a horrid day, haven't you? Come and sit down; I'll have supper on the table in no time. It'll be nice for you to have an outing and go and see those children again—she said that they still miss you.'

Lady Thorley phoned after supper; the children were well and getting on famously with Miss Thompson but they did want to see her again. Daisy agreed to go to tea on Saturday and was relieved and at the same time disappointed to be told that Lady Thorley would be on her own. 'Hugh won't be home until Sunday—we can have a nice gossip and I know Miss Thompson will be glad to see you again.'

Daisy put down the phone; the doctor would have got back to London by then, of course. A good thing too, she muttered to Razor as she gave him his supper.

She woke to rain on Saturday morning, not that she minded overmuch; for two days she was free of Mrs Brett's grumbling voice. She got the breakfast, saw Pamela off to spend the day with friends, made a shopping-list with her mother and walked to the centre of Wilton; doled out carefully, there was money enough to buy all the right sort of food; she visited the butcher, the grocer and the post office, bought bread still warm from the oven, and carried the lot home, had coffee with her mother and, since there were only the two of them, settled on soup and bread and cheese for lunch. While her mother got them ready, she went up to her room and changed into a navy blue jersey dress she had bought in the January sales. It was elegant, well cut and well made, and it fitted her nicely, but the colour did nothing for her. A well-meaning friend had once told her in the kindest possible way that unless a girl was pretty enough to warrant a second look it was wise to wear clothes which didn't draw attention to herself. Daisy, aware of her shortcomings, had taken her advice. Besides, one didn't get tired of neutral colours; at least, in theory one didn't. That she was heartily sick of them was something she never admitted to herself.

The twins would have been happy to see her wearing an old sack; they gave her a rapturous welcome and the welcome from Lady Thorley and Miss Thompson was equally warm. There was a good deal of talking before everyone settled down—Lady Thorley to go back to her drawing-room and Miss Thompson and the children, taking Daisy with them, to the nursery where she was shown the twins' latest craze. They had discovered the joys of Plasticine, which they had not been so keen on when Daisy had looked after them—not just small quantities of it, but large lumps which they were modelling into a variety of large and obscure objects.

'I'm no good at making things,' confessed Miss Thompson as they sat down at the table. 'I can just about manage a dog or a cat but Josh wants a model of Buckingham Palace.' She handed Daisy a hefty lump. 'They tell me that you're very good at making things...'

So Daisy embarked on the royal building while the twins, their tongues hanging out with their efforts, started on their various versions of the Queen and Prince Philip, all the while talking non-stop. Presently Miss Thompson said quietly, 'Daisy, I've some letters to post; would you mind very much if I go now? Josh and Katie are happy with you—if it weren't raining so hard we could all have gone...' Daisy didn't mind. At Josh's request she had stopped her modelling to make a drawing of Razor and she had no worries about keeping the children amused. The village post office wasn't too far away; Miss Thompson would be back in plenty of time for tea. Daisy glanced at the clock; she had promised to be home as soon after six o'clock as possible, but that was three hours away.

One drawing of Razor wasn't enough; she embarked upon a series of this splendid animal, handing over each sketch for the children to colour, Katie in her favourite pink, Josh with large spots and stripes. It was a good thing that Razor, a dignified animal, wasn't there to see.

She was putting the finishing touches to Razor's fine whiskers when she heard the twins give a kind of whispered shout, but before she could look up two large, cool hands covered her eyes.

'Guess who?' asked a voice she had done her best to forget.

There was no need for her to reply—the twins were shouting with delight, 'You don't know, do you, Daisy? You must guess—we'll help you...'

She should have been feeling annoyance but instead she felt a pleasant tingling from the touch of his hands and a distinct thrill at the sound of his voice. Which simply would not do. Besides, the children would be disappointed.

'Father Christmas?' she suggested, a remark hailed by peals of laughter from Josh.

'Silly Daisy, it's not Christmas yet,' and,

'Two more guesses,' said Katie.

'Mr Cummins?' She had heard all about him from the twins; he had been in the nursery all day repairing the central heating.

'One more,' shouted Josh.

'Dr Seymour.' Her voice was quite steady.

'You mean Uncle Val. You've guessed; now you don't have to pay a forfeit.'

'What a pity,' remarked the doctor and dropped his hands to let them rest on Daisy's shoulders, which she found even more unsettling. 'I don't mind being taken for Father Christmas but I'm not so sure about this unknown Mr Cummins.'

'The plumber,' said Daisy and wished he would take his hands away.

However, he didn't; indeed he began to stroke the back of her neck with a thumb, which, although wholly delightful, she soon put a stop to by getting up quickly; and, since she had no idea what she was going to do next, it was a relief when Miss Thompson, followed by Lady Thorley, came into the room.

'Shall we all have tea here?' asked Lady Thorley, and didn't wait for an answer.

'I'll tell Cook,' said Miss Thompson, leaving Daisy to clear the table of the lumps of Plasticine, fend off Boots's delighted caperings and find a cloth for the table. The doctor, sitting with a twin on either knee, listened to his sister's idle talk and watched Daisy.

Tea was noisy, cheerful and leisurely, and Daisy, despite the doctor's unsettling presence, enjoyed herself so much that she forgot the time, and, her eye lighting on the clock, she saw that it was already past six o'clock.

She caught Lady Thorley's eye. 'I really have to go,' she said. 'I said I'd be home by six . . .' She lifted Boots's great head off her lap and stood up as the twins raised a roar of protest. 'Look,' she told them, 'if your mother and Miss Thompson will allow it, you can come and have tea with me and meet Razor.'

'When?' asked Josh.

'Any Saturday.' She paused. 'No, not next Saturday; I have to work that day.'

She began her goodbyes, long-drawn-out on the part of the children, brisk and friendly from Miss Thompson, and was politely cool towards the doctor.

'I'll see you to the door,' Lady Thorley said comfortably and they went down the hall, lingering for a moment while Daisy got into her plastic mac and uttered suitable thanks. She had her hand on the doorknob when the doctor joined them, took her hand off the knob and opened the door.

'Ready?' he asked briskly, and to his sister said, 'I'll be back shortly, Meg.'

Daisy swept out into the porch, then found her voice. 'My bike's here—I'm cycling home—I can't leave it here, I need it . . .'

He had opened the car door and she found herself inside without quite knowing how she had got there. 'Your bike will be delivered to you at the latest by tomorrow afternoon, so stop fussing.'

He got inside the car, fastened her seatbelt as well as his own and made no effort to start the car.

'Enjoying your new job?' he asked.

She said peevishly, 'Oh, so you did see me the other day—you looked at me as though I weren't there. Thank you, I quite like the work; I like the patients too...'

'But?'

His voice was beguilingly encouraging and for a moment she forgot that she wanted nothing more to do with him. 'Mrs Brett—the other orderly—she's been there a long time and she's a bit set in her ways; I suppose she's seen so many patients she doesn't really notice them any more.'

'And what do you intend to do about that?'

'Me? Nothing. I've only been there for a few weeks and I want to keep the job; and besides, who am I to criticise her? Only I can see that the patients can reach their water jugs and cut up their meat and pick up their knitting.' She stopped and went a bright pink. 'That sounds priggish; I can't think why I'm telling you about it—it's not important.'

He said casually, 'Why not get a transfer to another ward?'

'Orderlies are sent to a ward and stay on it until they're moved somewhere else.' She stared ahead of her. 'I think we're called ancillary workers but we're domestics. When are you going back to London?'

The sound which escaped his lips might have been a chuckle. 'Very shortly; that's a relief, isn't it? We shan't need to ignore each other if we should meet at the hospital.'

There didn't seem to be a reply to that.

He drove her home then, carrying on the kind of conversation which meant nothing at all but sounded pleasant. He got out when they reached her home, opened her door and held the gate as she went through it.

She thanked him as he shut it behind her, making it obvious that if she had invited him in he would have refused anyway, so she wished him goodbye and went into the house.

'Is that you, darling?' called her mother from the kitchen. 'Are you very wet?'

'I got a lift,' said Daisy, getting out of the hated mac, 'and my bike will be brought back some time tomorrow.'

'Who brought you back?' Her mother had poked her head round the door to ask.

'Dr Seymour came to tea and brought me back.' She added quite unnecessarily, 'It's raining.'

Her mother gave her a thoughtful look. 'Yes, dear. I've started supper.' She opened the door wider. 'But I thought you might like to make the pie—all those apples and they won't keep.'

Daisy, rolling pastry ten minutes later, wondered if Dr Seymour was staying with his sister, and if not where was he? He must live somewhere. In London? He worked there too, didn't he? Perhaps he had a house there as well as living in Salisbury; but perhaps he didn't live there either.

She frowned, reminding herself that she had no interest in him.

Much refreshed by a weekend at home, Daisy went back to work on Monday, full of good resolves: not to allow Mrs Brett to annoy her, to carry out her orders even if she found them unnecessary—locker-tops didn't need to be washed twice a day, whereas water jugs, sitting empty, needed to be filled... She bade her superior good morning and had a grunted reply, followed by a stern request to get on with the cleaning since it was the consultant's round, 'And don't you hang around wasting time picking up knitting and such like, and see that the ten o'clock drinks trolley is on time; I don't want no 'itch.'

Daisy didn't want a hitch either; all the same she contrived to unpick a row of knitting and take two lots of hair curlers out while Mrs Brett had gone to have her coffee.

Her hopes of a better relationship between herself and Mrs Brett came to nothing; it seemed that she couldn't please that lady. Whatever she did was found fault with, and as the week progressed it was apparent that Mrs Brett had decided not to like her and nothing Daisy could do would alter that. They parted company on Friday evening with Mrs Brett full of foreboding as to how Daisy was going to manage over the weekend.

'You'll get no 'elp,' she warned her. 'You'll 'ave ter work for two, and lord knows what I'll find when I gets 'ere on Monday morning.'

Daisy said, 'Yes, Mrs Brett,' and 'Goodnight, Mrs Brett,' and cycled home, the prospect of two days without her surly companion quite a pleasing one.

Without that lady breathing down her neck every ten minutes or so, Daisy found herself enjoying her work; she had common sense, speed and a kind nature that, she discovered for herself, was what her job was all about. No one bothered her; she got on with her chores and found time to satisfy the needs of those patients who were not in a fit state to look after themselves. She went off duty on the Saturday evening feeling pleased with herself even though her feet ached abominably.

Sunday was even better, for Sister wasn't on duty until one o'clock and there was a general air of leisure on the ward so that there was time to listen to titbits of news read aloud by those patients who had the Sunday papers and pause to help with the odd crossword puzzle. She went down to the canteen feeling that life was quite fun after all.

She was going off duty that evening, crossing the main entrance hall, inconspicuous in her good suit, when she saw Dr Seymour watching her from one corner. He was talking to one of the house doctors, staring at her over the man's shoulder. She looked away at once and whisked herself out of the door and over to the bicycle racks and presently pedalled home as though the furies were after her, but no Rolls-Royce sped past her, and she arrived home out of breath and feeling foolish. What, she asked herself, had she expected him to do? Speak to her? Open the door for her? A thin-lipped smile perhaps?

She was free all day on Monday, a splendid opportunity to help her mother around the little house, tidy the garden before the weather worsened and change the library books. As she biked to work on Tuesday morning she allowed herself to wonder if she would see the doctor.

Scrambling into the pink overall in the small room the orderlies used, she was accosted by one of them. 'Lucky you,' said the girl, 'you're being sent to Children's—Irma told me—it's on the board outside. You'd better look for yourself.'

'Me?' said Daisy. 'But I thought you never got moved...'

'Someone off sick, I dare say—make the best of it, Daisy, it's the best ward in the whole place.'

There, sure enough, was her name—to report to the children's unit forthwith. She skipped along corridors and in and out of swing doors with a light heart; no more Mrs Brett . . . She was opening the last of the swing doors when she remembered that Dr Seymour was a consultant paediatrician.

CHAPTER SIX

AFTER the quietness of the women's medical ward, the children's unit gave forth a steady roar of sound: shrill cries, shrieks, babies crying and cheerful voices, accompanied by background music just loud enough to weld the whole into a cheerful din. Daisy paused just inside the doors, not sure where to go; there were doors on either side of the wide hall leading to the ward. She supposed she should report to Sister...

A very pretty young woman put her head round one of the doors. 'Our new orderly?' she asked in a friendly voice. 'Come in here, will you, and I'll give you a few ideas...?'

Sister Carter was as unlike Sister on Women's Medical as chalk was from cheese. Not much older than Daisy, with curly hair framing a delightful face, she looked good enough to eat. Daisy, bidden to sit, sat and said politely, 'Good morning, Sister. I'm the orderly; my name's Daisy.'

'Nice—the children will love it.' She glanced at a folder on her desk. 'I see you've been working in a nursery school, just the kind of person we need here.' She smiled at Daisy. 'Lots of dirty work, though.'

'I don't mind that, Sister.'

'Good. Come and meet Maisie—our other orderly.'

Maisie was on her hands and knees clearing up a toddler's breakfast porridge which had been hurled away in a fit of childish pique. She came upright, beaming from a round and cheerful face. ''E's at it again, Sister,' she observed without rancour.

'Naughty boy,' said sister. 'Maisie, here is Daisy, your new partner.'

''Ello, love, am I glad to see you—one pair of 'ands don't go far with this lot.' She looked Daisy over in a friendly way. 'Like kids?'

'Yes,' said Daisy.

'You and me'll get on fine,' declared Maisie. ''Elp me clear the breakfast things and I'll tell you what's what as we go.'

Daisy had never been so content; the ward was a happy place despite the sick children in it and she had spent the day clearing up messes, sorting clean linen and bagging mountains of soiled sheets and small garments, going to and fro with meals, making Sister's coffee and listening carefully to Maisie's advice. Maisie was a treasure with a heart of gold and endless patience. The nurses were nice too; she might not be one of them but she had been made to feel that she was part of the team. Daisy blessed the unknown authority who had seen fit to send her to the children's unit. Going down to her short tea break, she wondered who it was.

The unknown authority was sitting in Sister Carter's office, going over his small patients' case-sheets and drinking strong tea from a mug. Presently he glanced up. 'The new orderly—she'll settle down?'

'Daisy? Oh, yes, sir. A nice little thing. You recommended her, didn't you? Not quite our usual sort of girl but she has a way with the children and our Maisie assures me that she's a good worker. She's at tea—did you want to see her?'

'No. My sister employed her as nanny to her children and she needed to have a job near home. Now, what are we going to do with baby George? He had better have another X-ray. I have to go back to town this evening but I'll speak to Dr Dowling before I go—I shall be away for the rest of this week.' He got up to go. 'Thanks for the tea.' As he went through the door he saw Daisy's pink-clad person disappearing into the ward.

It was late evening when he left the hospital and drove himself through the city, through the medieval gates of the cathedral close and parked before his house. It was a very old house, but like many of its neighbours had a Georgian front with an important pillared door and a charming transom over it. He let himself in and was met in the hall by a tall, bony woman of uncertain years, whose sharp-nosed face lighted up at the sight of him.

'There you are, sir. And there's your dinner waiting for you, and eat it you must before you go to London... I've packed your case and there's messages for you——' She was interrupted by a deep-throated barking. 'That's Belle, in the garden with all the doors shut, but she knows it's you.'

'Sorry I'm late, Mrs Trump. Give me five minutes, will you? Thanks for packing my bag; I'll join Belle for a moment—I could do with some fresh air.'

The doctor opened a door at the back of the square hall and went into a fair-sized walled garden behind the house, to be greeted with ecstasy by a golden Labrador. He bent to fondle her ears and then strolled round the small garden still bright with autumn flowers until his housekeeper called from the door and they both went inside to the dining-room, its walls panelled, the mahogany table and sideboard gleaming with polished age, silver and glass gleaming in the soft light of the wall-sconces. He ate his solitary, deliciously cooked meal without waste of time, had coffee at the table and, accompanied by Belle, went to his study to collect up those papers he wished to take with him. It was a pleasant room at the back of the house, its walls lined with books, its leather chairs large. His desk was large too, every inch of it taken up with case-sheets, folders and a mass of reading matter. It looked a splendid muddle but he put his hand on what he wanted without hesitation, put it into his briefcase and went up to his room to fetch his bag.

Downstairs again, he went through the door beside the graceful little staircase and found Mrs Trump loading the dishwasher. He let Belle into the garden and addressed himself to his housekeeper.

'I'll be away for the best part of the week,' he told her. 'I'll ring you later.' He smiled at her. 'Take care of yourself.' He whistled to Belle and presently got into his car and drove himself away. It would be late by the time he got to London but the drive would give him time to think. Rather against his will he found he was thinking about Daisy.

Daisy was thinking about him too. She had been on tenterhooks all day expecting to see him on the ward, but there had been no sign of him, nor had his name been mentioned. 'And a good thing too,' she muttered to herself. 'The less we see of each other the better; he unsettles me.'

Luckily, when she got home her thoughts were happily diverted by a letter from Philip, home on leave in Bristol and asking if he might drive down to Wilton and see her. A day out together, he suggested in his neat handwriting, or failing that could they meet for a meal? If she would like that could she phone him and perhaps something could be arranged.

Her mother and Pamela, apprised of the contents of the letter, were enthusiastic. 'Phone him now,' urged Pamela. 'You're free this weekend, aren't you? Well, say you'll spend the day with him. Wear the good suit. Debenhams have got a sale on; see if you can get a top to go with it—one of those silk ones, you know, short sleeves and a plain neck; you can borrow Mother's pearls...'

Philip sounded pleased when she phoned. Saturday, he suggested with flattering eagerness. They could drive out into the country and have lunch. He assured her that he was looking forward to seeing her again and to exchanging their news. Daisy put down the receiver feeling a faint glow of pleasure.

Before she slept that night she lay thinking about Philip; it would be nice to see him again—he was a very pleasant companion and they got on well together, which thought somehow reminded her that she and the doctor didn't get on well at all. Surprisingly, it wasn't Philip in her sleepy thoughts, but Dr Seymour, his handsome face vivid under her eyelids.

Naturally enough, she saw no sign of him during that week. There were a number of children under his care and a youngish man with a friendly face came each day to see them. Daisy, cleaning the bathrooms with Maisie, asked who he was.

'E's Dr Dowling, registrar to Dr Seymour—keeps 'is eye on the kids when 'is nibs isn't here.' Maisie gave her a sidelong glance. 'Got a boyfriend, 'ave you, Daisy?'

'Me? No...'

'Go on with you, a nice girl like you.'

Daisy thought of Philip. 'Well, it's true, though I'm going out on Saturday with someone I met a little while ago in Holland. Just for lunch.'

'Holland, eh? Been to foreign parts, 'ave you? I've always fancied a bit of travel meself. Is 'e a Dutchman, then?'

'No, he just works there; he's on holiday.'

Maisie was mopping the floor. 'Our Dr Seymour, 'e goes over to Holland once in a while—very clever, 'e is, with the kids. Tells other doctors what to do.'

That sounded like him all right, thought Daisy, arranging the tooth-mugs in a neat line on their appointed shelf. She squashed an impulse to talk about him and instead suggested that she should go to the kitchen and get the trolley ready for the dinners. 'Unless there's something you'd like me to do first, Maisie?'

'You run along, Daisy, and get started, then, and lay up a tray for Sister at the same time, will you? She likes her pot of tea after her own dinner.'

Saturday came at last. Daisy got up early and dressed carefully. She had found a plain silk top to go with the suit, very plain, round-necked and short-sleeved, but if they were to go to the kind of restaurant where she would be expected to take off her jacket it would pass muster. The pearls gave it a touch of class, or so she hoped.

Carefully swathed in one of her mother's aprons, she got the breakfast, saw to Razor's food and sat down with her mother and Pamela to boiled eggs and bread and butter.

'Let's hope you get a smashing lunch,' said Pam with her mouth full. 'Any idea where you're going?'

'Not the faintest. If he hasn't been to Salisbury before I dare say he'll want to look round the cathedral.'

Pamela looked horrified. 'But that's not romantic.'

'I'm not expecting romance,' said Daisy. She had the ridiculous idea that if it were Dr Seymour and not Philip it would have been romantic in a coal hole. She frowned; really she was allowing the most absurd ideas to run through her head. She helped clear the table, made the beds and did her hair again and then went downstairs to wait for Philip.

He arrived punctually, greeted her with pleasure, drank the coffee her mother had ready and led the way out to his car. It was a small, elderly model, bright red and nice but noisy. Daisy got in happily enough. Philip had no wish to see the cathedral; instead he had planned a trip down towards the coast, through Fordingbridge and Ringwood. A friend of his had said that there was a good pub in Brockenhurst where they could have lunch. 'We could go on to Beaulieu but I don't suppose there would be time for that; I have to get back this evening.'

'Yes, of course; come home to tea, though.'

They were almost on the outskirts of Salisbury when the doctor, driving the other way, passed them. Neither of them noticed the Rolls slide past them but he, even in the few seconds allowed him, had a clear view of them both laughing.

Less than ten minutes later he drew up before her home, got out and banged the knocker. Mrs Pelham came to the door, beaming a welcome.

'How very nice to see you again!' she exclaimed. 'Did you want to see Daisy about something? Such a pity you've just missed her.' She opened the door wider. 'Do come in and have a cup of coffee; I've just made some.'

'That,' said the doctor at his most urbane, 'would be delightful. I'm on my way to see my sister.'

Mrs Pelham looked past him. 'Is that a dog in the car? Yours? Bring him in, do. Razor won't mind.'

'Her name's Belle; she's very mild. You're sure—er—Razor won't mind?'

'Our cat. He has a keen brain, so Daisy says, but he's bone-idle.'

They sat over their coffee, with Belle at her master's feet and Razor sitting on the corner of the mantelpiece for safety's sake, and since the doctor was at his most charming Mrs Pelham told him all about Philip coming to take Daisy out. 'All the way from Bristol,' she observed. 'They've gone down towards the coast—I told Daisy to bring him back for tea. He seemed a nice young man.'

'Indeed, yes,' agreed the doctor, at his most amiable. 'I met him while I was at the Hague—a sound young man.' He put down his coffee-cup. 'I must be on my way.'

It was only as he was at the door saying goodbye that he asked casually, 'Daisy is happy at the hospital?'

Mrs Pelham said happily, 'Oh, yes, and now she's been moved on to the children's ward—your ward?—I dare say you'll see her.' She hesitated. 'But of course she's an orderly; I don't suppose you talk to them.'

He said gravely, 'Well, I don't have much contact with anyone outside the medical or nursing profession. I must look out for her, though.'

'Yes, do,' said Mrs Pelham. 'I'm sure she'll be delighted to see you again.'

He agreed pleasantly, reflecting that delight was the last thing he expected to see on Daisy's face.

In the car, he assured himself that it was because Daisy was so unwilling to like him that he found her so often on his mind. She appeared to have got herself a possible husband too. There was nothing wrong with young Philip; he would be an ideal husband in many ways, reliable and hard-working with little time for romantic nonsense. 'Well, if that's what she wants...' he muttered so savagely that Belle lifted an enquiring ear.

It might have been a relief to the doctor's feelings if he had known that Daisy had never once thought of Philip as a husband. If she had had a brother she would have liked him to be just like Philip—easygoing and cheerful, a good companion. She was enjoying herself enormously; there was a great deal to talk about, mostly about his work in the Hague and his hopes for the future, and at Brockenhurst they had found the pub without difficulty and had a ploughman's lunch, and presently drove on to Lymington, parked the car on Quay Hill and walked the length of the High Street and then down to the shore to look at the sea.

'We must do this again,' said Philip as he drove back later. I've got two weeks. Are you free every weekend?'

'I have to work every fourth weekend. That'll be in two weeks' time—I've been sent to another ward and the off duty's different.'

'I'm going to Cheshire to spend next weekend with friends and I'll be gone before you get your next free weekend. Could I come and see you at the hospital?'

'Heavens no. I mean, not just like that—I suppose if something really urgent happened and someone needed to see me about something.' Daisy shook her neat head firmly. 'Otherwise not.'

'I'll be home for a few days for Christmas; we must see each other then.'

He gave her a brotherly grin and she said, 'Yes, that will be nice.'

They had a splendid tea with her mother and Pamela, and Mrs Pelham, if she hoped for signs of a romance, was very disappointed; nothing could have been more prosaic than Daisy's manner towards Philip, and he, thought Mrs Pelham sadly, was behaving like a brother.

He left soon after tea, unknowingly passing the doctor's Rolls once more in one of Wilton's narrow streets, happily unaware of the frowning scrutiny that gentleman gave him as they slowed, going in opposite directions. The doctor had spent several hours in his sister's company, had a civil conversation with his brother-in-law, obligingly played a rousing game of snakes and ladders with his nephew and niece and had pleaded an evening engagement as soon as he decently could, and now he was driving himself back to his house in the close. He had a consultation at the hospital on Monday morning and there was no point in going back to London. He had no engagement; at the back of his mind had been the tentative idea that it might be pleasant to take Daisy out to dinner and use his powers of persuasion to stir up her interest, even liking, for him. Only an idea and a foolish one, he told himself and greeted his housekeeper with tight-lipped civility so that she went back to the kitchen to cook an extra-splendid meal. 'To take his mind off things,' she explained to Belle, who was eating her supper under the kitchen table.

She might just as well have served him slabs of cardboard although he complimented her upon the good food as he went to his study, where he sat, Belle at his feet, doing absolutely nothing but think about Daisy.

It was a waste of time thinking about the girl, he reasoned; cold facts proved that. She had disliked him on sight, and she had even told him so, hadn't she? He was far too old for her and he was quite sure that if she were to discover that it was through his good offices that she had got work at the hospital she would quite likely throw up the job at once. As far as he knew, she had never discovered that it was he who had asked his sister to take her on as a nanny, nor did she know why she had been moved to the children's ward or who had arranged that. He hoped she never would. What had started as a kindly act towards a girl who had intrigued him had become an overwhelming desire to make life as easy as possible for her.

He went up to bed at last, long after midnight, resolved to put her out of his mind. There was more than enough to occupy it; he had his work, more than he could cope with sometimes, many friends and family; he would find himself a wife and settle down. The doctor, a man with a brilliant brain, a fund of knowledge and priding himself on his logical outlook on life, had no idea how foolish that resolve was.

As for Daisy, she had enjoyed her day. They had reminisced about the Hague, and she had listened to Philip's light-hearted criticism of his job, pointing out in a sisterly fashion that however dull it might be at the moment it could lead to an interesting post.

'Well paid too, I shouldn't wonder,' she had added.

'Oh, yes,' he had agreed. 'I don't do too badly now. They like married men for the more senior jobs, though the thing is to get promotion and find a wife at the same time.'

They had laughed together quite unselfconsciously about it.

She had settled down nicely on the children's ward; it was hard work and at times extremely messy but Sister Carter was a happy person and the ward and its staff took their ambience from her; the nurses were treated fairly and if there were any small crises—and there very often were—and it was necessary for them to work over their normal hours, she worked with them. Daisy, going about her lowly tasks, wished that she could be a ward sister. She was happy enough, however; she was on good terms with the nurses and Maisie and the children had accepted her as a familiar face.

The week went by without a glimpse of Dr Seymour and she didn't know whether to be pleased or vexed when she went back after the following weekend to hear from Maisie that he had been to the ward several times during the weekend but had now returned to London.

As casually as she could, Daisy asked, 'Does he only come at weekends?'

'Lord bless you, no—'e comes when there's something needs sorting out, too much for 'is registrar; 'e comes regular like, for 'is rounds and out-patients and that. Busy man, 'e is.'

It was her turn to work at the weekend and she couldn't entirely suppress a feeling of expectancy as she cycled to work. Maisie had said that the doctor sometimes visited on a Saturday or Sunday and there was a chance that he might as there were several ill children on the ward...

There was no sign of him on Saturday; the registrar had been to the ward several times, obviously worried about some of the children, and Sister, who was on duty for the weekend, had spent a long time at their cotsides. Daisy longed to know what was the matter with them and if Sister hadn't been so busy she would have asked. As it was, she was busy herself, managing to do Maisie's work as well as her own. Sunday was just as hectic too but in the early evening the children seemed better and the ward was quiet. Daisy could hear the distant continuous murmur of visitors on the floors below; in another hour she would be going home... She picked up the tray of tea she was taking to Sister's office and, pausing at its door, came face to face with Philip.

He said breezily, 'Hello, is this where Sister lives? I've come to see you—I'm sure she won't mind just for a few minutes; I brought a friend down from home to visit his granny—she's had an operation.'

'You can't...' began Daisy, but it was too late; he had tapped on the door and she heard Sister's nice voice telling whoever it was to come in.

Afterwards she tried to understand what had happened. Sister had looked up from her desk and she and Philip had just stared at each other; they looked as though they had just discovered something they had been searching for all their lives and for the moment she had been quite sure that neither of them had any idea of where they were or what they were doing. She had waited for a moment for someone to say something and then put the tray down on Sister's desk. Sister had moved then and so had Philip.

Philip spoke first. 'I brought someone to visit and I wondered if I might have a few minutes with Daisy— we met in Holland.' He held out a hand. 'Philip Keynes...'

Sister blushed. 'Beryl Carter. You're a friend of Daisy? It's not really allowed to visit staff, but since you're here...'

'It's not at all important,' said Philip, summarily dismissing Daisy from his mind and life without a second's thought, so that Daisy slipped away and fetched another cup and saucer. She was in time to hear Sister say,

'Do sit down, Mr Keynes; have you come far?'

Daisy had never quite believed in falling in love at first sight, but now she knew better. They would make a nice pair, she reflected as she helped a hard-pressed nurse to change cotsheets. Philip would have to get a larger place in which to live, of course—if he had a wife he might get his promotion. She was deep in speculative thought when Sister came to the ward door.

Philip was standing by the swing doors, ready to leave. He said in a bemused kind of voice, 'I say, Daisy, I'm so glad I came to see you.' Then when she agreed pleasantly he went on, 'She's got a day off tomorrow; I'm coming to take her out for the day...'

'What a splendid idea,' said Daisy. 'I'm sure you'll have a lovely time. She's so very nice, Philip.'

'Nice? She's an angel—I knew it the moment I set eyes on her.'

He was, she saw, about to embark on a detailed description of Sister Carter's charms. Daisy cut him short in a kindly way. 'Good for you; I must go. Let me know what happens next, won't you?'

She went back into the ward; there was still almost an hour before she was free to go home.

Sister was in the ward checking one of the ill children when Dr Seymour came quietly in. Daisy, going down the ward with an armful of nappies for one of the nurses, slithered to a halt when he came towards her. He gave her a cold look and she wondered why; she hadn't expected a smile but his eyes were like grey steel. Naturally enough, if she had but known, for he had seen Philip leaving the ward only seconds before he himself entered it. The young man hadn't seen him; indeed, he was in such a state of euphoria that he was in no shape to see anything or anyone. The doctor, his face impassive, entered the ward in a rage.

He was still there when it was time for Daisy to go off duty. She bade Sister goodnight, and whisked herself away. It was a pity that she was free the next day—Dr Seymour might still be at the hospital, although, if he was going to look at her like that, perhaps it was just as well that she wasn't going to be there. She frowned; the last time they had met they had been quite friendly in a guarded sort of way. She shook off a vague regret and fell to planning what she would do with her free day.

It was nice to have a day at home, to potter round the garden, help her mother around the house; do some shopping. After supper she sat down at her mother's desk and carefully checked their finances. There was very little in the bank but at least they were paying the bills as they came in and putting by a little each week into what she called their 'sinking fund', which really meant schoolbooks for Pamela, and for having shoes mended and what she hoped would be a winter coat for her mother. She went back to work on the Tuesday morning feeling that life wasn't too bad; a few months' steady work and it would be even better; further ahead than that she didn't care to look. The thought of being an orderly for the rest of her working days made her feel unhappy.

She was cleaning out the older children's lockers by their small beds when Dr Seymour came in. Sister was with him; so was Staff Nurse, his registrar, a young houseman and one or two persons hovering on the fringe whom Daisy couldn't identify. He brought with him an air of self-assurance nicely timed with a kindly, avuncular manner—very reassuring to his patients, reflected Daisy, getting off her knees and melting discreetly into the nearest sluice-room. Maisie had dinned it into her on her first day that orderlies kept off the wards when the consultants did a round.

Maisie was having her coffee break and the sluice-room was pristine; Daisy wedged herself near the door and watched the small procession on its way round the cots. It was a leisurely round; Dr Seymour spent a long time with each occupant, sometimes sitting on the cotside with a toddler on his knee. He had a way with children, Daisy admitted, making them chuckle and undisturbed when they bawled.

The group moved round the ward and crossed over to the other side to where the older children were and Daisy, getting careless, opened the sluice-room door a little wider just as the doctor came to a halt and looked up, straight across the ward and at her. His look was impassive so why did she have the feeling that he was laughing behind that blandness? She stared back, not sure whether to shut the door or melt into the sluice-room out of sight, or perhaps stay well out of sight where she was.

The problem was solved for her, for he moved away, his head bent to hear what Sister was saying.

She had been at home for half an hour that evening when the doorknocker was soundly rapped. Pamela was in her room doing her homework, her mother was making a shopping-list and said vaguely, 'The door, dear,' so Daisy, spooning Razor's supper into his saucer, put the tin down and went to see who it was.

Dr Seymour stood on the doorstep and at her startled, 'Oh, it's you,' wasted no time on polite preliminaries.

'I should like a word,' he told her, and since he expected to be invited in she stood on one side.

'Come in, Dr Seymour.' Her voice was tart for she saw no reason to be anything else. Why he should want to come and see her was a mystery—surely if she had needed a reprimand for something she had done wrong on the ward it should be Sister who administered it?

She opened the sitting-room door but he brushed past her. 'You're in the kitchen?' he said, and before she could answer he had stalked in, to wish her surprised mother good evening with just the right degree of apologetic charm.

Mrs Pelham put down her pencil. 'Dr Seymour—how nice. Do you want to talk to Daisy? I'll make a cup of coffee.' She smiled at him in her gentle way. 'Do sit down.'

He sat, refusing the coffee at the same time. 'I've come to ask a favour of Daisy.' Since she was still standing just inside the door, he got up again. Lovely manners, reflected Mrs Pelham and told Daisy quite sharply to sit down. It would be easier to talk to him sitting down; he loomed rather large on his feet . . .

'My sister asked me to come and see you; she's unable to leave the children. Miss Thompson has had to go home to look after her sick mother and she thinks that I can explain matters more easily than if she spoke to you on the telephone. She and her husband have to attend some function or other next Saturday evening. There is no one she cares to leave the children with; she'll have to take them with her. She hopes that if you're free you might be persuaded to go with her and look after them— just for Saturday and Sunday. They'll take you up in the car and bring you back, of course.' He looked at Daisy. 'Of course we realise that it is an imposition; you have little enough free time. But the children like you and Meg trusts you, Daisy.'

Daisy opened her mouth to say no and then closed it again. After all, he was only passing on a message from his sister; it was really nothing to do with him, and Lady

Thorley had been very kind to her. She glanced at her mother who smiled faintly at her. 'Why not, dear?' asked her parent. 'It will be a nice little change for you, and Lady Thorley has always been so kind to you.'

Daisy still hesitated, though; indeed she might have refused if Pamela, hearing voices, hadn't come down to see who had called. Her hello was casually friendly. 'I bet you want to borrow Daisy,' she said, and pulled up a chair to the table. 'Do tell. What is it this time? Measles?'

The doctor laughed. 'Nothing to do with me; I'm only the bearer of a message. My sister wants Daisy to go with her and the children to London for the weekend— their governess has had to go home for a few days.'

'Good idea; will you drive her up?'

'I—no, no. I shan't be here. My sister would fetch Daisy if she's willing to go.'

'Of course she'll go,' said Pamela, 'won't you, Daisy?'

Daisy, unable to think of any reason to refuse, said that yes, she would.

He got up to go presently, saying all the right things before going to the door with Daisy. As she opened it he asked carelessly, 'Have you seen any more of young Philip?'

He gave her a friendly smile and she quite forgot that she had no wish to be friendly too. 'Oh, yes, he came to see me the other evening; he met Sister Carter, though.' She forgot for the moment to whom she was speaking. 'It was really very strange—I mean, they just looked at each other as though they had known each other all their lives. I've never believed in love at first sight, but now I do.'

She glanced at him and saw the little smile and felt her cheeks grow hot. 'Goodnight, Dr Seymour,' she said coldly and opened the door wide.

His, 'Goodnight, Daisy,' was uttered with great civility and he said nothing else. She stood at the door, keeping still and not looking as he got into his car, and as he drove away closed it with deliberate quiet. Otherwise she would have banged it as hard as she was able; she had made a fool of herself talking to him like that. He would be sitting in his car, smiling that nasty little smile... her face was scarlet at the thought.

The doctor was indeed smiling, a slow, tender smile which made him look years younger. He drove to his sister's house, whistling softly under his breath, and Belle, sensing that he found life very much to his satisfaction, sat on the back seat and thumped her tail happily.

CHAPTER SEVEN

THERE was no sign of the doctor when Daisy went to work in the morning and she wasn't sure whether to be relieved or disappointed. Dr Dowling did a ward-round with the housemen and staff nurse, since Sister Carter had a day off—out with Philip, no doubt of that. Daisy wondered where they would go—somewhere romantic, she hoped. Maisie, bustling up and down the ward, gave her opinion that Sister was far too pretty to be stuck in a hospital. 'Ought to 'ave a 'ome of her own with kids.' She gave a hoarse chuckle. 'And that won't be no trouble to 'er—she's 'ad enough practice 'ere.'

At home, Daisy combed through her wardrobe again. She supposed it didn't really matter what she wore when she went to London, and it was only for two days anyway. It would have to be the good suit once again; she could travel in a blouse and take the silk top, spare undies and night things and her small collection of make-up. They could all go easily enough into the roomy shoulder-bag, which would leave her arms free for the twins.

'You don't suppose you might get asked out?' asked her mother hopefully.

'No, love. I shall be with the twins while the Thorleys go to this banquet or whatever it is. I dare say I shall take them for a walk in the morning and we'll come back here in the afternoon. I shall enjoy the trip there and back,' added Daisy in her sensible way.

'Where will you stay?'

'Don't know. In a hotel, perhaps, or they may even have a flat or house in London—that's the most likely, I should think.'

'It sounds rather dull to me,' observed Mrs Pelham. If Daisy agreed with her parent she didn't say so.

Sister Carter was on duty the next morning, starry-eyed and looking prettier than ever. During the morning she sent for Daisy to go to her office, and when she tapped on the door and was bidden to enter she was told to sit down.

Daisy sat composedly while she beat her brains trying to remember if she had done something worthy of a talking-to. So it was all the more surprising when Sister Carter said cheerfully, 'Philip was telling me about you yesterday. You really shouldn't be an orderly, you know, Daisy. Can't you train as a nurse?'

It was so unexpected that Daisy didn't answer at once. When she did her voice was as quiet as usual. 'I think I might like to do that, Sister, but until my sister is through school I do need to have a job; a student nurse's pay wouldn't be quite enough . . . besides, I—I need to live at home.'

'For how long would that be?' asked Sister Carter kindly.

'Another three years. There would still be plenty of time for me to train as a nurse—I'm twenty-two—I wouldn't be too old . . .'

She was uttering a pipe-dream—her mother couldn't be left alone and Pamela would be miles away at some university, but there was no need to burden Sister with that.

'A pity. Still, there doesn't seem to be anything we can do about it at present, does there? As long as you're happy here?'

'I am—very happy, Sister.' That at least was true, thought Daisy.

'Well, we'll have to see,' said Sister Carter vaguely. She smiled suddenly. 'I don't suppose I'll be here in three years' time, but I'll make sure that you have a special splendid reference when I go.'

She hesitated. 'Did you have no opportunity to train for anything, Daisy?'

'No, my father died.'

'I'm sorry. Anyway, you can count on me if ever you see the chance to start training.'

Back in the ward, bagging the endless nappies, Daisy thought it unlikely.

Saturday came, bringing with it chilly blue skies and a sunshine without much warmth. Just the right weather for the suit, decided Daisy, getting up early.

Lady Thorley arrived late, explaining worriedly that the twins had been troublesome at the last minute. 'If you wouldn't mind sitting in the back with them, Daisy?' she asked. 'They're cross because we haven't brought Boots with us.' She added hopefully, 'They usually listen to you.'

At first they weren't disposed to listen to anyone, even Daisy whom they liked, but presently they decided to be good and the rest of the journey was made in comparative harmony. All the same Daisy was relieved to see the outskirts of London closing in around them; there was so much more to see and the children, rather excited now, were kept busy pointing out everything which caught their eye. Daisy was excited too although she appeared serene enough, as Lady Thorley drove along Millbank and the Victoria Embankment until she turned off at Northumberland Avenue, skirted Trafalgar Square and turned into Pall Mall, and after that Daisy was lost— she didn't know London well; all she knew was that they had crossed Piccadilly and were driving through streets of dignified mansions opening out from time to time into quiet squares encircling a railed-off garden. Very pleasant to sit there under the trees on the wooden seats, thought Daisy, and indeed there were small children and mothers and nursemaids doing just that. Living in such surroundings it would be hard to remember that the busy London streets were close by.

Lady Thorley drove past another square and turned into a tree-lined street where the houses were smaller, although to Daisy's eyes they looked of a handsome size, and presently stopped halfway down the terrace.

'Well, here we are,' Lady Thorley observed. She looked over her shoulder to the twins. 'You've both been very good—are you tired, Daisy?'

'Not in the least, Lady Thorley. Would you like me to see to the cases or mind the children?'

'The children, please; Trim will take the bags inside.'

The house door had opened and an elderly man, very spry, crossed the pavement.

'Trim, how nice to see you again. Will you see to the luggage for us? This is Miss Daisy Pelham who has kindly come with me to look after the children.'

Trim greeted her with dignity, exchanged a more bois-terous greeting with the children and took the car keys from Lady Thorley. 'Nice to see you again, my lady,' he said. 'Mrs Trim will be waiting for you.'

The door opened on to a small vestibule which in turn led to a long wide hall. Daisy, following Lady Thorley indoors, saw that the house was a good deal larger than it appeared to be from the outside but she had little time to look around her. Advancing to meet them was a stout middle-aged woman with improbable black hair and eyes to match. She had a round face which crinkled nicely when she smiled and the children rushed towards her with shouts of delight.

'There, my darlings—you've grown, I declare.' She embraced them and swept towards Lady Thorley. 'Welcome, my lady. Your usual room and I've put Miss Pelham next to the children.' She turned a beady eye on Daisy and smiled largely. 'You'll be wanting to see to them. If you, my lady, would go to the drawing-room while I show Miss Pelham their rooms? There will be coffee in a few minutes and lunch is at one o'clock.'

She bustled Daisy and the children up the elegant staircase at one side of the hall, along a narrow passage and into a room at its end. 'The children usually sleep here.'

It was a large room with two beds and white furniture geared to suit a small person and a big window over-looking a surprisingly long, narrow garden at the back of the house. 'You will be here, Miss Pelham.' The housekeeper opened a door and Daisy walked past her into a charming room, the bed and dressing-table in maplewood, a comfortable little chair by the window and a matching tallboy against one wall. The bedspread and curtains were in a faint pink and the carpet underfoot was a deep cream and very soft.

'The bathroom is here,' said Mrs Trim, throwing open another door, 'if you won't mind sharing it with the children.'

Daisy nodded wordlessly and Mrs Trim trotted to the door. 'You'll want your coffee. It'll be downstairs in the drawing-room; the twins know where that is.'

Left with the children, Daisy made haste to see to their wants, brush their hair, apply handkerchiefs to small noses, and urge them to good manners when they went downstairs while she tidied her already neat head, powdered her prosaic nose and added lipstick. That done, she led the way downstairs again. In the hall she said, 'Josh, dear, which is the drawing-room?'

He took her hand and the three of them opened the door to which he led them. Lady Thorley was sitting there comfortably by a small fire in a handsome Adam fireplace but for the moment Daisy only had eyes for the room. It was of a comfortable size, its bow window overlooking the street and it was furnished with what she recognised as antiques. Beautiful cabinets, lamp tables, a long sofa table and in one corner a long-case clock was tick-tocking in a soothing monotone. The chairs were large, upholstered in wine-red velvet, and there were two sofas, one each side of the fireplace.

'There you are,' said Lady Thorley. 'Daisy, come and have some coffee; you must be parched. Josh, Katie, Mrs Trim has made some lemonade especially for you. Sit down by Daisy and drink it up.'

Over coffee Lady Thorley voiced her plans for the evening. 'This banquet is at nine o'clock but there's a reception first and that's at eight o'clock. We shall have to leave here about a quarter past seven. Would you see that the children have their suppers and go to bed? Mrs Trim will have a meal ready for you about eight o'clock. We shall be very late back so go to bed when you want to. In the morning would you give the twins their breakfasts and have yours at the same time and perhaps take them for a walk for half an hour or so? I expect lunch will be at one o'clock and we'll leave about three o'clock. Hugh's coming back with us, so he'll drive, thank goodness.'

Daisy took a sip of coffee. It was delicious. 'Very well, Lady Thorley. I could have supper with the children if that would be more convenient.'

'No, no. You deserve an hour or two of peace and quiet. Trim will look after you.' She glanced at the clock. 'Lunch must be almost ready.'

She looked across at the children, one each side of Daisy, drinking their lemonade with deceptive meekness. 'Now you must behave nicely at table...'

'If they don't,' said the doctor from the door, 'I shall throw them into the garden—not you, of course, Daisy.'

He strolled into the room, kissed his sister's offered cheek, suffered an excited onslaught from his nephew and niece and wished Daisy a bland good-day. 'You had a good trip?' he asked. 'Hugh should be here at any minute; I'll tell Trim to serve lunch ten minutes after he gets here—that will give us time for a glass of sherry.'

Daisy hadn't uttered a sound. She was surprised and delighted and at the same time puzzled; he had spoken as though he owned the place...

He caught her eye. 'Welcome to my home, Daisy,' he said and smiled with such charm that she blinked her lovely eyes and went pink.

'You've gone all red,' said Josh but before his mother could reprimand him Sir Hugh joined them and in the general hubbub and the handing of drinks Daisy was able to regain her normal colour and during lunch she was far too busy seeing that the children ate their meal and behaved themselves to feel self-conscious. The doctor's manners were impeccable; whenever possible he included her in their conversation but beyond polite answers she took little part in it, which gave her the chance to look around.

The dining-room was behind the drawing-room, overlooking the back garden. Here again was a bay window with a door leading to a covered veranda. The walls were panelled and hung with paintings, mostly portraits, and the table and sideboard were mahogany of the Regency period. The table had been decked with a damask cloth, crested silver and crystal glasses. The soup was served in Worcester plates, as was the ragout of chicken, and, as a concession to the children's presence, the trifle, with glacé cherries and whipped cream. The twins spooned their portions up without any urging and were bidden by their uncle to sit still while Daisy had her coffee. She didn't linger over it; she felt sure that the three of them had plenty to talk about. She excused herself, removed the children from the table and bore them off upstairs where they were prevailed upon to lie on their beds while she told them a story. They were asleep within ten minutes, looking like two cherubs, leaving her to sit by the window with nothing to do. Presently, lacking anything to keep her awake, she closed her eyes and dozed off.

She woke to find the doctor sitting on Josh's bed, a twin on either side of him. All three of them were watching her with unnerving intensity.

'You were snoring,' said Josh.

'I never snore,' declared Daisy indignantly, very conscious of being at a total disadvantage.

'No, no, of course you don't.' The doctor was at his most soothing. 'Josh, no gentleman ever tells a lady that she snores—it's bad manners.'

Daisy sat very upright. 'I'm sorry I went to sleep...'

'No need to be sorry. I expect you were up early and two hours or more of these children, mewed up in a car, is sufficient to make anyone doze off. But we're glad you're awake. We wondered if you would like to come with us—we're going to take a quick look at the zoo.' He glanced at his watch. 'It's not yet three o'clock—we could have an hour there and come back for a late tea.'

He didn't wait for her to agree. 'If you could get these two ready, and yourself, of course, and come downstairs in ten minutes or so, I'll have the car outside.'

He had gone before she had said a word.

For once the twins were both quick and helpful; with a minute to spare they were downstairs in the hall where they found the doctor talking to his sister.

'Splendid, you're ready. Meg, we'll be back around five o'clock—tell Mrs Trim to have tea ready for the children, will you? Ask for yours when you want it.'

He ushered his party outside, shovelled the children into the car and told Daisy to get in beside him. 'A pity Belle can't come too...'

'Oh, is she here? I haven't seen her.'

'She has been with me all the morning—she's in the garden now; you'll see her when we get back.'

The streets were comparatively empty, and the distance wasn't great; beyond the excited chatter of the twins, little was said. Once there, they lost no time in deciding what had to be seen in the time they had.

'Snakes and scorpions, sharks and man-eating tigers,' demanded Josh, to be instantly contradicted by his twin.

'Bears and elephants,' she demanded, 'and a camel.'

'Well, I dare say we shall have time to see all of them, provided you don't hang around too long. Let's get the snakes and scorpions over first, shall we?'

Daisy, annoyed at the high-handed way in which the doctor had arranged her afternoon without so much as a by your leave, found her annoyance melting in the face of the children's happy faces and his whole-hearted enthusiasm for the afternoon's entertainment. The snakes and scorpions duly shivered over, the bears admired, the camels marvelled at, there was time to have a ride on an elephant. The twins weren't faint-hearted; they needed no one with them, they assured their uncle and Daisy watched the great beast with its burden of small people plod away.

'They'll be all right,' she breathed anxiously. 'They're so small, though...'

'Well, of course they're small; they're children, aren't they?' The doctor sounded testy. 'Do you suppose I should allow them to go unless I was quite certain they would come to no harm?'

'Well, no,' said Daisy placatingly, 'I'm sure you wouldn't.'

He looked down at her. 'How's the job going?'

'Very well, thank you.' She considered telling him that Sister Carter had mentioned her training to be a nurse, but decided not to—it might sound a bit boastful.

'I suppose you won't be there long,' he said airily, a remark which sent her into instant panic.

'Oh, why not? Aren't I suitable? I know I'm not as quick as Maisie...'

'Suitable? Oh, you're that all right. I was merely uttering my thoughts aloud.'

He said no more, leaving her to wish that he would keep his thoughts to himself.

The children came back then and there was no chance to ask him what he had meant. With the promise that they should come again next time they came to London, the twins were stowed in the car and, with a silent Daisy beside him, the doctor drove back to his house. It was a crisp winter evening and Daisy thought longingly of tea and was delighted to find that Mrs Trim, mindful of the twins' bedtime, had set out a splendid meal in a small room at the back of the house. It was a very cosy room, with a bright fire burning, plenty of bookshelves and comfortable chairs as well as the round table loaded with the twins' favourite food, a pot of tea for Daisy and a dish of little cakes.

Lady Thorley joined them for a moment. 'I'm just off to dress,' she told Daisy. 'We shall have to leave in an hour or so—you'll be all right? I know Val has told the Trims to look after you. We shall be late back, I expect.'

She embraced her children. 'I'll come back and tuck you up before we go,' she promised, 'and so will Daddy.'

The children were nicely tired and, after a splendid meal, sleepy. Daisy led them away upstairs, undressed them, and urged them, rather reluctantly, to their baths. They were emerging from these noisy and damp activities, the twins with shining faces and smelling of the best kind of soap, and Daisy dishevelled and damp, when their parents and the doctor came to say goodnight. Lady Thorley, in sequinned black chiffon, looked superb, as did Sir Hugh in his white tie and tails, but it was the doctor who stole the show; he wore his evening clothes with ease and elegance, his broad shoulders enhancing the inspired cut of his coat, the very size of him meriting a second or even third glance. Daisy took one look and turned her head away because he was watching her with that small smile which she found so disconcerting. There was no need to look at him again; she was fully occupied in keeping the twins from embracing their mother too fervently.

'If you get into your beds,' she suggested in her calm fashion, 'I dare say everyone will kiss you goodnight.' She added artfully, 'And there'll still be time for another chapter of *The Rose and the Ring*.' This was a book to which they were passionately devoted and which Lady Thorley had had the presence of mind to bring with her.

Soothed by their favourite story, the children presently slept and Daisy went down to the quiet dining-room and found Trim waiting for her.

'A glass of sherry, miss—little Josh and Katie can wear you out.' When Daisy hesitated he added, 'The doctor said you should have a glass before your dinner, miss.'

'Oh, did he?' asked Daisy. 'How kind of him. In that case I'd like one.'

Presently Trim led her to the table. At the sight of the damask and silver and crystal, for all the world as though the table had been decked out for a dinner-party, Daisy exclaimed, 'Oh, but you shouldn't have gone to all this trouble! I could have had something on a tray.'

'The doctor wished it, miss,' said Trim, 'and I must add it is a pleasure for us. Mrs Trim has cooked a meal which she hoped you will enjoy.'

He disappeared and returned presently with vichyssoise soup, and Daisy's small nose wrinkled at its delicious aroma. It tasted good too—this wasn't something out of a tin, it was the real thing, made with cream and eggs and chicken stock nicely mingled with the creamed leeks. It was followed by a perfectly grilled sole, sautéd potatoes and braised celery, and when Trim offered her white wine she accepted, quite carried away by the unexpectedness of it all.

'Mrs Trim's special sweet,' murmured Trim, removing her empty plate and offering a chestnut soufflé with chocolate cream, 'and I shall serve your coffee in the drawing-room, Miss Pelham.'

When she hesitated again he added, 'The doctor hoped that you would keep Belle company for a little while.'

'Well, just for a short time,' said Daisy, 'and do please thank Mrs Trim for that delicious meal.'

Belle was delighted to see her and accompanied her on a tour of the room. There was a lot to see: fine porcelain and silver in their display cabinets and a great many paintings, mostly portraits. She supposed that they were of the doctor's ancestors, for several of them had his dark hair and heavy-lidded eyes, even the suspicion of the smile which made her feel so uneasy.

An hour passed quickly and when the case clock chimed a tinkling half-hour she bade Belle goodnight and went into the hall. Should she go to bed without telling Trim? she wondered. Would he mind if she went in search of him through the baize door at the end of the hall? As if in answer to her problem Trim appeared silently from the dining-room, asked if there was anything she required, wished her goodnight and informed her in a fatherly way that should the children wish to get up early either he or Mrs Trim would be about in the kitchen should they require a drink of milk before their breakfast.

Daisy thanked him, wished him goodnight and went to her room. The twins were fast asleep; she bathed in peace, got into her own deliciously comfortable bed and closed her eyes. Before she dozed off she wondered what the doctor was doing and whom he might be with. Some lovely young woman, she thought forlornly, dressed with the same expensive taste as Lady Thorley. She was too tired to wonder why the thought made her unhappy.

She was wakened by the twins who had climbed on to her bed and were whispering into her ear, urging her to wake up. 'We want to go into the garden with Belle,' Josh explained.

Daisy sat up in bed, tossing back her mousy curtain of hair. 'Isn't it a bit early? Wouldn't it be nice if you got under the eiderdown and I read a bit more of *The Rose and the Ring*?'

Katie liked the idea but Josh thrust out his lower lip and shook his head. 'I want to go into the garden...'

'So you shall presently, love, but it's only just after six o'clock; it isn't even quite light...'

'Belle wants to go too.' He fixed her with a very determined eye. 'We're going home today and she won't see us again.'

'Oh, I'm sure she will; your uncle often goes to see you. You stay here with Katie like a good boy and I'll fetch your book.'

The house was pleasantly warm and the carpet was soft under her bare feet when she got out of bed and went in search of the book—a matter of a minute or so, but when she got back Josh wasn't there.

'Josh says he's going out into the garden,' said Katie. 'I think I'll go too.'

'We'll all go,' said Daisy desperately, 'only give me time to get some shoes on his feet and his dressing-gown on. Stay there, darling—I promise we'll all go if you do.'

Katie had made a tent of the eiderdown and was prepared to stay. Daisy flew out of the room and down the stairs, guided by the murmur of Josh's voice, to be halted at the bottom step by the doctor's voice. He was leaning over the banisters watching her with interest.

'Good morning, Daisy,' he observed in the mildest of voices. 'A pleasant surprise so early in the day...'

'Oh, be quiet, do,' said Daisy waspishly. 'Josh is going into the garden and he's only in his nightclothes...' It was borne in upon her that she was in a like state and she wasn't wearing sturdy winceyette pyjamas.

The doctor had come down the stairs, wearing a rather splendid dressing-gown and soft slippers. He hadn't been told to be quiet for a very long time and certainly not by a small girl in her nightie; he found it intriguing. He said, with a glance which reassured her that he hadn't even noticed what she was wearing, 'I'll get him out of the kitchen and bring him back to you. Get the pair of them dressed and we'll all go into the garden.'

Daisy was already halfway up the stairs but she turned round to whisper fiercely, 'But aren't you tired? Don't you want to go back to bed?'

'Yes to both questions. Just do as I say, there's a good girl.'

She opened her mouth to tell him that she wasn't his good girl but thought better of it and he went on down the hall to the baize door.

Katie was delighted as Daisy told her of the prospect of a walk in the garden with her uncle. 'I'll dress you in a minute,' declared Daisy, tearing into her clothes, washing her face and cleaning her teeth and tugging a comb through her hair. She looked a fright but at least she was decent... Katie, for once, was only too glad to be dressed too; Daisy was fastening her shoes when the doctor, bearing a tray of tea and two mugs, closely followed by Josh and Belle, appeared silently at the door.

He had them all organised within minutes. The children were to drink their milk and Josh was to get into his clothes as far as he was able, 'And Daisy and I are going to enjoy a cup of tea.'

Belle had got on to the bed beside Katie and since the doctor didn't seem to mind Daisy said nothing but meekly took the cup of tea she was offered and drank it.

'Put on something warm,' advised the doctor, finishing his tea. 'I'll be with you in ten minutes.'

Daisy still said nothing; it was hardly an occasion for aimless conversation and she was feeling shy because of the inadequacies of her nightie. The doctor took his vast person silently away and she set about rearranging Josh's clothes in the right order—jersey back to front, shoes on the wrong feet and childish hair standing up in spiky tufts all over his small head.

She had time to tie her hair back before the doctor returned and they all crept downstairs and, with Belle in close company, out into the garden through the kitchen door. It was chilly with a hint of frost still in the air but the sun had almost risen by now and the birds were singing. No one, thought Daisy, would know that they were in the heart of London, standing in the quietness.

She wasn't allowed to stand for long. The doctor took her arm and urged her along the flag-stoned path between a wide border—herbaceous in the summer? wondered Daisy, being whisked briskly past—and a strip of lawn which took up the whole of the centre of the garden. The path disappeared behind shrubs and ornamental trees, ending in a charming little rustic hut with an arched door and tiny windows on either side of it.

'The witch's house,' explained the doctor as the children tumbled inside. He pushed her gently before him and then followed her so that they were a bit crowded. There were benches built along its walls and he sat her down and then folded his great size into the space beside her. The children had no intention of sitting;

they were exploring the little place as they always did, finding plates in a shallow opening in the wall. Everything was taken down, examined and put back again until presently Josh came to stand by Daisy.

'She's a good witch,' he explained; 'she's kind to animals and children and if she casts a spell it's a nice one.'

'She sounds a very good sort of witch; does she have her meals here?'

Josh, carried away on childish imagination and with Katie playing dutiful chorus, went into some detail while the doctor watched Daisy's face. It was alight with interest and the practical suggestions she offered as regards the witch's diet showed that she was entering whole-heartedly into the children's world. He sat back, enjoying himself.

Presently he said, 'We'd better go back for our breakfasts.' So the children put everything neatly back in place and they all went back into the garden, out of the shrubs and the small trees, on to a similar path on the opposite side of the lawn with an identical flowerbed against one high brick wall. The sun was up now but held little warmth and the children danced to and fro with Belle weaving between them.

'You have a very charming garden,' said Daisy, for something to say.

'A bonus in London. The house has been in the family for many years—George the Fourth's time, I believe, and in those days gardens were considered small. Be that as it may, it's secluded and quiet.'

She took the children upstairs to wash their glowing little faces, brush their hair and tidy them for breakfast, a meal they shared with the doctor and their father. Lady Thorley was having hers in bed.

The two children, perched each side of Daisy, ate their meal in an exemplary fashion, calling forth praise from their parent. 'We're going home directly after lunch,' he told them. 'What do you want to do this morning?'

'A ride on the top of a bus,' said Josh, as usual speaking for Katie as well as himself, and when neither gentleman reacted with enthusiasm to his suggestion it was Daisy who said,

'Oh, what a splendid idea. If you tell us which bus to catch and what time we're to be back here...'

She was disappointed that the doctor had made no offer to go with them. Their father, she guessed, would want to remain with his wife, but surely the doctor could have spared an hour or so...

'There's a sightseeing bus goes from Trafalgar Square—I'll drop you off,' said the doctor casually. 'I won't be able to pick you up when you get back but take a taxi, Daisy.' He glanced at her. 'Have you enough money?'

She flushed. Somehow he had made her sound like a servant.

'I've no idea what it will cost, but I don't expect I have.'

Sir Hugh took out his wallet, found some notes and handed them over. 'That should cover it. If you're short, we can settle with the cab when you get back.'

The two men sat back, looking as though they had settled the matter to their satisfaction, and since the children were getting restless Daisy excused herself and them and took them upstairs to get them ready for their trip. Ten minutes later, without seeing anyone, the three of them left the house. The doctor had said he would give them a lift to the bus, but she hadn't believed him; it shouldn't be too difficult to find a bus stop and get to Trafalgar Square.

He was leaning against the car's gleaming side, obviously waiting for them. Belle was already on the back seat and the children lost no time in joining her; unlike Daisy, they had had no doubt in their minds that if their uncle had said he would do something it would be done.

The doctor opened the car door. 'You didn't believe me, did you?' He sounded mildly mocking as she went pink.

'Well, no. You must have got home very late in the night and you were up early this morning.'

He had got in beside her. 'And how very worthwhile that was,' he observed softly. And she, remembering, blushed.

An episode to be forgotten, she told herself as the three of them sat perched on the top deck of the bus and she pointed out the House of Commons, Westminster Abbey, Buckingham Palace, the Tower of London and all the other sights on the route. The children looked when bidden but like all small children were far more interested in the people on the pavements and the other traffic. Culturally, the trip hadn't been very successful although they had enjoyed every minute of it and at lunch they gave colourful accounts of people they had seen: the policeman, the horse guards, several ambulances, flashing blue lights and racing through the traffic, plenty of policemen on motorbikes, and a small crowd surrounding a man who had fallen down in the street. Their sharp eyes had missed nothing.

'Did you see Buckingham Palace?' asked their father.

'Where's that?' asked Josh.

'Anyway, they enjoyed their morning,' said their mother comfortably.

The doctor had little to say; only when his sister put a low-voiced question to him did Daisy realise that he had been at the hospital. He would be glad to see the back of them, she reflected. She stole a look at him and decided that he looked tired; the twins, as she knew to her cost, could be exhausting and they had begun their day very early.

She repacked their bags after lunch, dressed the children in their outdoor things once more and collected her own possessions while the Thorleys stowed everything in the boot and made their farewells. No mention was made of the doctor returning to Salisbury; he took leave of them cheerfully on his doorstep, his hand on Belle's collar, and his polite, 'It was a pleasure,' was the only answer Daisy got to her thank-you speech.

She got into the car between the twins, telling herself that she never wished to see him again.

CHAPTER EIGHT

THE twins were peevish and inclined to quarrel and Daisy breathed a sigh of relief as Sir Hugh drew up before her home. She bade the twins a brisk goodbye, assuring them that they would see each other again, responded suitably to Sir Hugh's thanks and Lady Thorley's heartfelt gratitude and got out of the car.

'We will keep in touch,' declared Lady Thorley. 'We won't stop now—the twins...'

'I quite understand, Lady Thorley.' Daisy saw ominous signs of temper in the children's small faces and felt sympathy for their mother. They would be a handful by bedtime. She went through the gate and watched the car drive away and then went indoors.

There was no one at home, only Razor, who lifted a welcoming head and went to sleep again. Her mother, said the note on the table, had gone to church and Pamela was spending the day with her best friend and wouldn't be back until eight o'clock. Daisy took her bag upstairs, took her coat off and then made herself a cup of tea and laid the table for supper. Her mother would have had nothing much to eat since Pam hadn't been at home; she poked her nose into the fridge and set about gathering the ingredients for a Spanish omelette.

'You're back,' said Mrs Pelham, letting herself in half an hour later. 'Darling, I couldn't remember when you said you'd be home so I thought I'd go to Evensong. Have you been in long?'

She sniffed the air. 'Something nice for supper? What a dear you are; what would I do without you?'

Over the meal Daisy told her about her weekend; it didn't amount to much when all was said and done and her mother listened eagerly. 'Dr Seymour seems such a kind man; tell me some more about his home—it sounds lovely.'

Pamela came in presently, wanting to talk about her day with her friend and for the moment the doctor and his house were forgotten; only later, as Daisy got ready for bed, she allowed her thoughts to dwell on him.

She didn't see him until the end of the next day. She had been to tea and when she returned to the ward he was there, standing halfway down it talking to his registrar and Sister. His back was towards her, his hands in his pockets, crushing his long white coat, looming head and shoulders above his companions. Daisy paused just inside the door, staring at his vast back; she didn't know why, but she was sure that he was bone-weary although there was no sign of that, and she had a great urge to do something about it—a sensation which welled up inside her and left her feeling breathless, and what breath she had left her entirely when he turned his head and looked at her. She knew what the feeling was then. It was love, catching her unawares, and it couldn't have been at a more awkward or inappropriate time, nor could she have been more surprised. She wanted to smile with the sheer delight of it but his look was grave and thoughtful, reminding her that just for a moment she had imagined herself in a fool's paradise, so that she looked away and hurried down the ward to the far end to where she could see Maisie stuffing the day's dirty laundry into sacks. She felt terrible; a quiet corner, preferably in the dark with the door locked, where she could have a good weep in comfort, would have been just the thing. As it was she picked up an empty sack and began on the cotsheets.

Maisie didn't pause in her work. 'What's eating you?' she wanted to know. 'Look as though you've 'ad a nasty dream—white as them sheets, you are.'

'I'm fine,' declared Daisy. 'I've a bit of a headache...'

''Eadaches is useful things sometimes,' said Maisie. 'Make 'an 'andy excuse. Dr Seymour's back. Looks tired, 'e does too. All this to-ing and fro-ing don't do 'im no good. Can't think why he wants ter do it—'e's got 'is nice 'ouse in the close—what more could a body want?'

'Oh, I didn't know he lived in Salisbury as well as London.'

'Got a posh 'ouse there too, so I've heard. Not that I grudge 'im that. Does a lot of good, 'e does.' Maisie tied the strings of the last sack. 'I think 'e's gone—good. We'll get rid of this lot and go 'ome.'

Leaving the hospital presently, Daisy peered cautiously around her; there was no sign of the Rolls-Royce, nor its owner. The doctor had parked it behind the hospital and was standing at a ward window, watching her. He grinned tiredly, for she was craning her neck in all directions before getting on to her bike and pedalling way out into the busy street. He had wanted to walk down the ward and take her in his arms but even if that had been possible he was sure that she was still not quite certain of her feelings.

He turned away from the window and dismissed her from his mind.

As for Daisy, she cycled back home, her head in the clouds; it was one thing to find herself in love and quite another thing wondering what to do about it. Common sense dictated that to find work which would take her as far away as possible from the doctor was the thing to do but the very thought of not seeing him again sent such a strong shudder through her person that she wobbled dangerously on her bike. On the other hand, would she be able to bear seeing him at the hospital? Not speaking to him, of course, not even smiling, and probably in the course of time he would marry...

She wheeled her bike through the gate and into the garden shed behind the house and went in to find her mother rolling pastry.

Her, 'Hello, darling,' was cheerful. 'Pasties for supper and the gas bill came this morning, not nearly as much as we expected. I must say life is much easier now that you've got this job. You should be doing something better, I know—perhaps later on...'

Daisy kissed her mother, took off her outdoor things and gave Razor his supper. She said cheerfully, 'That's great about the gas bill. I'll pay it as I go to work—put it through the door; it'll save postage.'

'Had a nice day, dear?' asked Mrs Pelham.

Daisy gave the answer expected of her and reflected that unless she could find a job as secure with the same wages as she now had she would have to stay at the hospital. She would talk to Pam and see if she would look for a part-time job during the Christmas holidays. If only they could save a little money...

'You're very quiet, love,' observed her mother. 'Perhaps you're tired?'

It was Pamela, while they were washing up the supper things, who asked, 'What's up, Daisy? Is that job awful? Shall I leave at the end of term and get a job? It's so unfair that you should have to keep us going.'

'Don't you dare suggest such a thing—another couple of years and you'll be well on the way to a career and then it'll be your turn. And the job's not bad at all; in fact I quite enjoy it—the children are fun and the nurses are friendly.'

'Yes? All the same, you look different. Are you sorry about Philip?'

'Heavens, no. I liked him but that was all. He and Sister are so exactly suited to each other. I'm hoping to hear any day now that they're engaged.'

Pamela piled the plates neatly. 'All the same, there's something.'

Daisy wiped the bowl and wrung out the dishcloth. 'There's some money to spare—the gas bill's much less than we reckoned. There's the end-of-term disco…would you like something to wear?'

'No—you have it.'

'Shall we take Mother to Salisbury next Saturday and let her choose?'

'Is it enough for a dress?'

'Afraid not—a blouse from Marks and Spencer, or some slippers—hers are worn out…'

'OK,' said Pamela wistfully. 'Do you suppose there'll ever be enough money for us to go into a shop and buy something without looking at the price ticket?'

Daisy had picked up Razor and he lay across her shoulder, purring. 'Well, of course—just give me time to find a millionaire and marry him.'

Pamela laughed with her but she looked at her thoughtfully at the same time; Daisy's laugh had sounded a little hollow.

There was no Maisie when Daisy came to work the next morning. 'It's not like her,' commented Sister. 'I've never known her miss a day. I hope she's not ill—she's not on the phone.'

It was Staff Nurse who said, 'Probably she's overslept or been to a party...'

As the day wore on there was still no sign of her. Towards the late afternoon Sister sought out Daisy.

'I've got Maisie's address—I ought to go and see her myself but Philip's coming this evening.'

Daisy looked at the pretty worried face and said at once, 'I'll go on my way home, Sister. Probably it's nothing to worry about. I've got my bike and it won't take me long.' At Sister's relieved sigh she asked, 'Where does she live?'

It wasn't far out of her way—one of the little streets she passed each day turning off Fisherton Street. 'If I could ring my mother and tell her that I'll be home later?'

'Yes, yes, of course. Daisy, I'm so grateful.'

Maisie lived in a row of terraced houses at the very end of a narrow street, dwindling into a kind of no man's land of abandoned houses, old sheds and broken-down fences. She leaned her bike against dusty iron railings and thumped a dirty brass knocker.

She had to wait before someone came to the door—a young woman with her hair in pink plastic rollers, in a T-shirt and leggings and with a grubby baby under her arm.

'Good evening,' began Daisy politely and remembered that she had no idea what Maisie's surname was. 'I've called to see Maisie—she does live here?'

'Course she does. Miss Watts. Front room upstairs. 'Aven't seen her all day.'

The narrow hall was dark, so were the stairs. There were three doors on the small dark landing; Daisy knocked on the one facing the street and when no one answered tried the handle. The door opened under her touch and she found herself in a small room, surprisingly light and airy and smelling strongly of furniture polish.

'Maisie?' Daisy crossed the room to the bed along one wall where Maisie was sitting up against her pillows; she looked flushed and ill and took no notice of Daisy. There was a tabby cat curled up beside her and a small, scruffy dog on her feet. The dog growled as Daisy bent over Maisie and bared elderly teeth but Daisy was too concerned at the sight of Maisie to worry about that.

'Maisie,' she said urgently, 'what's the matter? Do you hurt anywhere? Did you fall down?'

Maisie opened her eyes. 'Pain in me chest,' she mumbled. She put out a hand and touched the cat. 'Look after 'em, Daisy...'

A doctor, thought Daisy, or better still get her to hospital where everyone knew her. 'And the animals... they need their suppers,' muttered Maisie.

There was a curtained-off alcove where Maisie had her kitchen; Daisy found cat and dog food kept there, piled it into bowls, filled a dish with water and gave Maisie a drink. 'I'm going to get a doctor,' she told her. 'I must go away for a little while and phone. I'll be back.'

There was a phone box further up the street and she rang the children's ward because she wasn't sure what else to do and since Maisie worked there surely someone would get her into hospital.

Sister was still on duty; Daisy didn't waste words. 'Sister, I'm so glad it's you. Maisie's ill. She has a pain in her chest; she looks awful. What shall I do?'

'Stay with her, Daisy; I'll get an ambulance organised as quickly as I can. Has she had a doctor?'

'No, I don't think so...' She rang off and hurried back, to find Maisie lying exactly as she had left her. The dog and cat had eaten their food and got back beside her, and Daisy rather warily picked up one of Maisie's limp, sweaty hands and found her pulse. It was very rapid and faint and Maisie seemed to be asleep even though from time to time she coughed painfully.

Daisy pulled up a chair, wiped Maisie's hot face with a damp cloth and sat down to wait. Sister would send help but it might take at least ten minutes, perhaps longer than that, before an ambulance arrived. Perhaps she should have dialled 999 first...

The door behind her opened quietly and she turned round; if it was the young woman who had let her in she might know who Maisie's doctor was.

Dr Seymour came hurriedly into the room. 'I was with Sister when you phoned,' he said in his calm voice which instantly soothed her worst fears. 'The ambulance is on its way. Has Maisie a doctor?'

'I don't know. There's a woman downstairs who let me in; she might know.'

'Don't bother. We can sort that out later.' He was bending over Maisie, taking her pulse, talking gently to her and getting a mumbled response.

'You're going to be all right, Maisie,' he assured her with calm matter-of-factness. 'You're going to hospital presently and we'll look after you.'

Maisie opened her eyes and caught at his arm. 'Milly and Whiskers——' she stopped to cough '—I can't leave 'em.'

'I'll take them home with me until you're well again.'

'Promise.' Her eyes sought Daisy. 'You 'eard what 'e said, Daisy? They're all I've got...'

'Don't worry, Maisie; if Dr Seymour says he will look after them, he will. All you have to do is get well again.'

The ambulance came then and after a brief delay while the doctor took the cat and dog out to his car and shut them in Maisie was borne away to hospital. The doctor had gone down with the ambulancemen and presently as she tidied the room and stripped the bed of its bedclothes Daisy heard it drive away. The room needed to be cleaned and there was food in the cupboard which would have to be either given or thrown away and she had better see the woman downstairs and then lock the door.

The doctor came soundlessly into the room. 'Maisie will go to the women's medical ward—virus pneumonia—I've warned them.' He looked round the room. 'We must do better than this when she's well again. Leave it all now, Daisy. I'll see that someone comes in in the morning to clear up. Perhaps you'll be good enough to come with me and give a hand with those animals?'

'My bike's here. And where are they to go?'

'To my house, of course. God knows what Belle will say when she sees them.' He took the key from the door. 'Come along, there's nothing more you can do here.'

He ushered her out on to the landing, locked the door and followed her downstairs, to knock on the nearest door. The young woman opened it, eyeing him with a slow smile. 'Got rid of 'er, 'ave you? Poor cow...'

'Miss Watts,' said the doctor evenly, 'has been taken to hospital; she is a much liked member of the staff there. We're taking her cat and dog with us and will care for them and in the morning someone will come and clear out Miss Watts' room. One more thing—is there someone here capable of riding a bicycle to Wilton? This young lady will be going back there by car later but she'll need the bike in the morning.'

He put a hand in his pocket and took out a note.

'Me 'usband'll do it—give us the address.'

The doctor was writing in his notebook and tore out the page. 'Your husband... he's here?'

A young man came to the door. 'OK, I 'eard it all. I'll ride the bike back—I've 'ad an 'ard day's work too.'

'Perhaps this will compensate for that,' said the doctor, handing over the note and the address. 'It's very good of you and I'm much obliged.'

'A doctor, are you?'

'Yes, indeed I am.'

The man laughed. 'A good idea to keep on the right side of the medics; you never know.'

'Be sure if ever you or yours should need our attention, you shall have the best there is,' said the doctor gravely and bade the pair of them goodnight before ushering Daisy out to the car.

The animals were sitting on a blanket on the back seat, looking utterly forlorn, and the sight of them was just too much for Daisy. Two tears trickled down her cheeks as she sat rigidly staring ahead of her while the doctor drove back into the heart of Salisbury and in through the entrance to the cathedral close. She hadn't said a word; she was beyond words—everything had happened so quickly and she seemed no longer capable of doing anything for herself.

The doctor hadn't spoken either although she knew he had seen the tears, but as he drew up before the house he handed her a beautifully laundered handkerchief, and waited while she mopped her face. Without looking at her he said in a matter-of-fact voice, 'Will you carry the cat? We'll take them straight to the kitchen and see if Mrs Trump can find them some food; Maisie has obviously cared for them but I suspect that she hasn't felt up to feeding them since she fell ill.'

Daisy said in a watery voice, 'I gave them something—Maisie was so worried about them.'

'Very sensible.' His manner was nicely detached and the brief glance he gave her was somehow reassuring. Perhaps she didn't look quite as frightful as she felt.

He got out of the car, opened her door and reached for the cat. It wriggled half-heartedly as Daisy took it in her arms and the dog, tucked under the doctor's arm, made no sound although it quivered. 'Poor little beast,' said the doctor and fished in his pocket for his keys.

His housekeeper came through the baize door as they went in and he said at once, 'Good evening, Mrs Trump. We have two lodgers to keep Belle company for a few days. Their owner is ill.'

Mrs Trump's sharp nose quivered but she said in the mildest of voices, 'I dare say they'll want a bite to eat, sir...?'

She glanced at Daisy, standing tidily beside the doctor, and he said, 'And this is Miss Daisy Pelham whose sensible help led to the patient being admitted to the hospital.' He swept Daisy forward, a great arm on her shoulders. 'Daisy, this is Mrs Trump, my housekeeper and long-standing friend.'

Daisy offered a hand and smiled and Mrs Trump smiled back, shook the hand firmly and asked, 'What about your dinner, sir?'

'Oh—stretch it for two if you can, Mrs Trump. Miss Pelham will be dining here before I take her home.'

A piece of high-handedness which Daisy had her mouth open to censure, to be stopped by his casually friendly, 'You will, won't you, Daisy? We must discuss what's to be done with Maisie. You shall telephone your mother in just a moment.'

He took the cat from her with the remark that he would only be a moment, and went through the baize door followed by his housekeeper, to return almost immediately, which gave her no time to gather together her scattered wits.

'Let me have your jacket.' He unbuttoned it and threw it over a chair before she could speak. 'Now come into the drawing-room and phone your mother.'

His large gentle hand propelled her through the door and into a room which took her breath away. There were tall windows and a door leading to the garden at the back and a wide arch opposite leading to the dining-room at the front of the house. There was a brisk fire burning in a burnished steel grate with a massive sofa on either side of it and a satinwood sofa table behind each of them. The walls were hung with burgundy silk and the ceiling was strapwork. There was a William and Mary winged settee by the window with a tripod table with a piecrust edge beside it and above a hanging cabinet with a delicate lyre pattern. At the other end of the room was a small grand piano, several winged armchairs grouped around a Regency library table and in the corner a wrought-iron stand holding a great bowl of chrysanthemums.

Daisy revolved slowly, taking it all in. 'What a very beautiful room,' she observed. 'Your London house is grand and beautiful too but this is like home...'

'As indeed it is.' He picked up the phone and dialled her home number and handed it to her, walked to the door to let Belle in from the garden and stood there with his back to her.

'Mother,' said Daisy and waited patiently while Mrs Pelham asked a great many agitated questions. 'No, I'm quite all right; Dr Seymour will bring me back presently. Yes, I know a man brought my bike home—I shall need it tomorrow. I'll explain when I get home; I'm quite all right—really. Now bye.' She hung up and the doctor came back from the window and offered her a seat on one of the sofas. He sat down opposite her with Belle's great head on his shoes.

'I'll drive you home when we've had dinner,' he told her. 'I'll take a look at Maisie later on once she has been settled in bed and tomorrow I'll get Dr Walker to look her over. If it is virus pneumonia—and I'm sure that it is—she can have a course of antibiotics and a week or ten days in hospital and then some sick leave. But you must agree with me that some other place must be found for her. That room was terrible.'

'It was spotlessly clean,' said Daisy. 'Bed-sitting rooms cost an awful lot of money, you know.'

He got up and went to a side-table with a tray of drinks on it. 'Will you have a glass of sherry?' He turned to smile at her. 'You look as though you could do with it.'

She felt her cheeks grow hot; she must look awful, hair anyhow and probably a red nose from crying. 'Thank you,' she said primly, and he hid a smile.

'I'll ask around; I'm sure there must be somewhere more suitable than her present room. You don't know if the furniture is hers?'

'No, I don't, but I think perhaps it is, because it was all so beautifully polished...' She sipped her sherry. 'What about Milly and Whiskers?'

'Oh, they can stay here. Mrs Trump has a heart of gold, Belle will be delighted to mother them and they can enjoy the garden.'

'But you're not always here.' She wished she hadn't said that because he smiled and didn't reply and that made her feel as though she had been nosy. The silence went on for a little too long and she was racking her brains for a suitable remark when Mrs Trump came to tell them that she had put the soup on the table. 'Those two poor creatures are asleep in front of the Aga,' she told them. 'Fair worn out, they are.'

The table was decked with the same elegance as that of his house in London; the doctor seated her, took his own chair at the head of the table and politely offered salt and pepper. They weren't needed; Mrs Trump was quite obviously the kind of cook whose food needed nothing added. The soup, served in Worcester china, was a creamy blend of leeks and potato with a hint of sorrel; Daisy, who cooked very nicely but of necessity dealt with the plainest of food, supped it with delight and wondered what would come next.

The plates were removed and the doctor engaged her in small talk and offered her white wine. Fish or chicken, she decided, agreeing pleasantly that Salisbury was a lovely city. It was roast duck, something she had never tasted before and it was delicious. She had known about the orange sauce but there was a delicious tang to it as well; if ever she had the chance, which wasn't likely, she would ask Mrs Trump what it was...

It was followed by castle puddings, served with a custard so rich that it must have been made almost entirely from cream. She refused a second helping and said rather shyly, 'That was the most delicious meal I've ever tasted.'

'Mrs Trump is a splendid cook and I must agree with you—what's the food like at the hospital?'

'Really very good—of course, cooking for several hundred people can't be the same as cooking for one, can it?' She thought for a moment. 'Besides, it's cabbage and mince and boiled potatoes, though we do get fish on Fridays and sometimes roast meat.'

She stopped then, afraid that she was boring him. 'If you don't mind I think I should go home...'

The doctor hadn't been bored; he had been sitting there, watching her nice face, listening to her pretty voice and thinking how delightful she looked sitting at his table, but he allowed none of this to show.

'Coffee? We'll have it in the drawing-room, take a quick look at Maisie's animals and then I'll drive you back.'

Daisy had had a long day; her eyelids dropped as she drank her coffee and the doctor bent forward gently and took the cup and saucer from her. She looked exactly right, sitting there in a corner of the sofa. Her small nose shone, the lipstick had long since worn off and her hair needed a good brush; moreover her gentle mouth had dropped very slightly open so that what sounded very like a whispered snore issued from it. Nevertheless her small person had an endearing charm. He touched her shoulder gently and she opened her eyes.

'I went to sleep,' said Daisy prosaically. 'I'm so sorry— it was the wine and the sherry. Whatever must you think of me?'

She sat up very straight and the doctor decided not to answer that. Instead he said soothingly, 'You must be tired. I'll take you home—are you on duty in the morning?'

'Yes. Please may I see the animals before we go so that I can tell Maisie how well cared-for they are?'

'Of course. We'll go now.'

Milly and Whiskers were curled up in front of the Aga in the kitchen—an apartment which Daisy considered to be every woman's dream. They eyed their visitors warily for a moment but Daisy got down on her knees and stroked their elderly heads and mumbled comfortingly and they closed their eyes again. 'I'll take care of them, don't you worry,' Mrs Trump assured her.

The doctor drove Daisy back in a comfortable silence, got out and knocked on her door, assured Mrs Pelham that there was nothing to worry about and wished Daisy goodnight.

She put out her hand. 'You've been awfully kind, sir. Thank you for my dinner and for seeing to the animals. Will Maisie be all right?'

'Yes. I can promise you that. Goodnight, Daisy.'

He had gone and she went indoors and sleepily told her mother and Pamela what had happened. It was

Pamela who told her to go to bed. 'You're tired out, aren't you, Daisy? And I suppose you've got to go to work in the morning?' When Daisy nodded she added, 'Do go to bed now—I'll see to laying the table for breakfast and feeding Razor. You would have thought they would have given you a day off...'

'Well, if Maisie's not there there's only me,' said Daisy and went thankfully to her bed.

She went to see Maisie the following morning during her coffee break. Feeling a good deal more self-possessed than on the occasion of her first visit to the women's medical ward, she tapped on Sister's door.

That lady said grudgingly, 'Ah, Daisy. I've been instructed to allow you to visit Maisie whenever it's convenient.' She lowered her head over the papers on her desk. 'She's at the end of the ward.'

Daisy met Mrs Brett halfway down the ward. 'And what are you doing here?' demanded her erstwhile colleague.

'Visiting,' said Daisy sweetly and walked past.

Maisie was sitting up in bed, looking a lot better than she had done the evening before. All the same, she was a shadow of her former cheerful self.

'Hello, Maisie,' said Daisy cheerfully, 'you look better already. I may come and see you whenever I have the time. I thought you'd like to know that Milly and Whiskers are fine. Dr Seymour's housekeeper is such a nice person and I'm sure she'll look after them.'

Maisie nodded her head. ''E came ter see me last night. I wasn't feeling too good but 'e said 'e'd look after 'em. What about me room?'

'Dr Seymour told me that he'd see about it so I shouldn't worry about it. Is there anything you want?'

'Me nighties and me 'andbag.'

'I'll get them for you this evening as I go home. Will it be all right if I bring them in the morning?'

'Yes, ducks.'

The unbidden thought crossed Daisy's mind as she left the ward that it would have been nice to see the doctor, but there was no sign of him. She went back to her work, doing her best to do Maisie's share as well and a little to her surprise getting some willing help from the nurses. All the same she was tired when she finished work for the day and got on her bike. It wasn't until she was knocking on the door of the house where Maisie had been living that she remembered that the doctor had locked the door of her room and probably there wasn't another key. She would have to ask the young woman if there was another one.

There was no need. 'Go on up,' said the young woman wearily, 'the door's open. Any more of you, are there? I don't aim to be opening the door all night.'

Daisy murmured apologetically and went up the stairs and opened Maisie's door. The doctor was there, sitting in one of the chairs, doing nothing.

'Oh,' said Daisy, aware of a rush of feeling at the sight of him. 'I didn't know—that is, Maisie asked me to get her handbag, only when I got here I remembered that I hadn't a key...'

He had got to his feet and took the key out of his pocket. 'I went to see her this afternoon and she told me and since I have the key I thought I'd better come along with it. By the way, Mrs Trump tells me that one of her friends is a widow living in Churchfields Road. She wants to let part of her house; I thought we might go along and see her. Tomorrow evening?'

'Me?'

He was lounging against the back of a shabby armchair, watching her. 'I feel certain that you know better than I what kind of a place Maisie would like.'

'Does she know? I mean, will she mind?'

'I suggested that it might be nice for her to move from this place, somewhere where there was a garden for Milly and Whiskers. She'll be in hospital for ten days; if we could get her settled before then she could go there and have some sick leave.' She was surprised when he said unexpectedly, 'How are you managing, Daisy?'

'Me? Oh, fine, thank you; the nurses are being marvellous and I believe there's someone coming to help part-time until Maisie's back.' He nodded and she went on, 'Don't let me keep you; if you'd let me have the key...'

'Anxious to be rid of me?' he said, but he said it kindly and smiled so that she found herself smiling back. 'Pack up whatever she needs and I'll take them back with me.'

She had found a large plastic bag and was collecting things from the chest of drawers; she put in all the things she thought Maisie might want and laid the handbag on top. 'But you haven't got the car here.'

'Ten minutes' walk.' He took the bag from her and opened the door. Locking it behind him, he said, 'I'll be outside tomorrow evening. We'll go in the car for I have an engagement later on. Leave your bike at the hospital—you can come in by bus in the morning?'

'Yes.' She had followed him down the stairs and the young woman poked her head out of a door and demanded to know how many more times they intended coming. 'The rent's paid until the end of the week—I shall let the room unless I get it by Saturday.'

'The furniture is Miss Watts'?'

'Yes, but not the carpet or the lights. Moving out, is she? I shan't be sorry—her and her animals. Don't know why I've put up with them all this time.'

'Someone will come here tomorrow to remove the furniture. Perhaps you would be good enough to be present when that is done. Good evening to you.'

He propelled Daisy out on to the pavement and the door banged shut behind them. 'You're never to come here alone, Daisy,' said the doctor firmly. 'I'll attend to whatever has to be done. Now get on your bike and go home.'

He waited while she unlocked the bicycle. 'Goodnight, Daisy.' His kiss was unexpected so that she almost fell off her bike. She muttered something and pedalled away from him at a furious rate. She heard him laugh as she went.

CHAPTER NINE

DAISY worried about that laugh all the way home. What had there been to laugh about? Did she look comical on a bike? Had she said something silly? With an effort she dismissed it from her mind. His kiss was harder to dismiss but then by the time she had reached her home she had convinced herself that it had been a casual gesture of kindness, rather like patting a dog or stroking a cat. She wheeled her bike into the shed and went in through the kitchen door.

Pamela was at the kitchen table, doing her homework, and her mother came from the sitting-room as she took off her jacket.

'Darling—you're so late again, I was getting worried.'

'I'll be late for the next few days, until we get some help instead of Maisie, Mother. I had to go to Maisie's room and get something for her.'

'You never went all the way back to the hospital?'

'No, Dr Seymour was there; he took it back for me.'

She saw the pleased speculation on her mother's face and sighed soundlessly; her parent was indulging in day-dreams again. Such hopeless ones too.

'What a kind man he is and you see quite a lot of him, don't you, love?'

'No,' said Daisy matter-of-factly, 'only if it's something to do with Maisie. He's asked me to go and look at a room to rent for her—she can't possibly go back to that awful place. I thought I'd go tomorrow after work.'

She wasn't going to mention Dr Seymour again; it would only add fuel to the daydreams.

Pamela was watching her thoughtfully. 'Lady Thorley phoned. She's asked you to go to tea on Saturday. I said you'd give her a ring.'

'Then I'd better phone her now...'

'Your supper's in the oven; I'll have it ready when you've done that.' Her mother peered anxiously at the cottage pie. 'We've had ours.'

'It's Miss Thompson's birthday—we thought we would give her a tea party. I'll come for you about three o'clock,' said Lady Thorley when Daisy duly phoned her. She had taken it for granted that Daisy would go and she agreed readily. It would be nice to see the twins again, and the proposed shopping trip to Salisbury with her mother and Pamela could wait.

She left the ward half an hour later than usual the next day—there was still no help and she had tried her best to do the work of two. Besides, she had gone to see Maisie in her dinner-hour, which had meant gobbling down Monday's mince and carrots and missing the pudding. She was in no mood to go anywhere but she had promised the doctor, and she wasn't a girl to break a promise lightly.

He was standing by the entrance, talking to the senior consultant physician, but they broke off their conversation to watch her cross the hall. Both gentlemen greeted her politely and the other man wandered away, leaving Dr Seymour to urge her through the door and into the car.

'Busy day?' he wanted to know.

'Yes,' said Daisy baldly.

'You've seen Maisie?'

'Yes. She's better, isn't she?'

'Yes. You went in your dinner-hour?'

'Yes.' Daisy felt that her conversation hardly sparkled but she was too tired to bother.

'You're bound to be hungry.' He picked up the car phone. 'Mrs Pelham, I'm just taking Daisy to look at rooms for Maisie—I dare say you know about that?' He was silent for a moment and Daisy wriggled with embarrassment; her mother would be explaining that her dear daughter, while mentioning that she would be late, hadn't said that he would be with her.

Dr Seymour's voice took on the soothing tones so effective with his small patients. 'I'll bring her back in the car, Mrs Pelham, you've no need to worry.'

He put the phone down and started the car without speaking and Daisy looked out of the window and wished that she were anywhere but there.

The drive was a short one; the quiet street he stopped in was lined with neat terraced houses with front gardens and well-kept front doors. He got out of the car and opened her door, remarking easily, 'This looks more like Maisie, doesn't it? We shall see...'

The door was opened the moment he knocked and the plump middle-aged woman said at once, 'Dr Seymour? Mrs Trump told me. Come on in.'

She looked enquiringly at Daisy, and the doctor said, 'This is Miss Pelham, who works with Miss Watts—I thought that perhaps she might know better than I...?'

He smiled gently and Mrs King smiled back. 'Of course.'

She nodded at Daisy in a friendly fashion and led the way into her house. The room they were shown into was exactly right, thought Daisy, and a door at its end led into a small conservatory which opened out on to quite a long garden, well-fenced. There was a gas fire and a very small gas cooker and a washbasin in one corner.

'Before my husband died he was ill for quite a long time, so we had this room specially done for him—there's a shower-room at the end of the hall. I never use it so it could go with the room. She's got her own furniture?'

The doctor had gone to look at the conservatory; obviously he expected Daisy to arrange things. 'Yes, she has. She has a dog and a cat too, both used to living indoors. You wouldn't mind?'

'As long as they don't bother me. A good dog would be quite nice to have—I'm a bit nervous, especially at night.'

'It's a very nice room,' said Daisy. 'I'm not sure if Maisie could afford it...'

'At the hospital, isn't she? Mrs Trump told me what she earned. Would she consider...?' She paused and then mentioned a sum a good deal less than Daisy had expected.

'I should think she could manage that. Could I let you know tomorrow? I shan't see her until then.'

The doctor didn't turn his head. 'Never mind that, Daisy. Would a month's rent in advance be acceptable?'

Driving back to Wilton presently, Daisy asked, 'Wasn't that a bit high-handed, Dr Seymour? How do you know that Maisie will like the room?'

He said placidly, 'If you were Maisie, would you like the place?'

'Oh, yes...'

'There's your answer.'

He stopped the car outside her home and got out to open her door.

'Thank you for bringing me home,' she told him and opened the gate.

'Your mother asked me if I would like a cup of coffee,' he said at his most placid, giving the knocker a brisk tattoo.

Pamela opened the door. 'Come on in,' she invited; she stood aside to allow him to pass her. 'The coffee's ready and Mother's bursting with curiosity.'

Her mother had got out the best china and there was a plate of mince pies on the table. The doctor took off his jacket and sat down, very much at his ease, answering Mrs Pelham's questions with every appearance of pleasure. Anyone looking at them sitting around the table, thought Daisy, would have considered him to be an old friend of the family.

Presently he got up to go and somehow it was Daisy who saw him to the door. 'I'll see Maisie in the morning but I'd be glad if you'd visit her if you can spare the time, convince her that she'll have a comfortable home and that it'll be much better for Milly and Whiskers. Once she has agreed I'll arrange to have her furniture moved in.'

'Very well,' said Daisy sedately, anxious to appear detached but willing. It was disconcerting when he patted her on the shoulder in an avuncular manner and observed that she was a good girl before bidding her a brisk goodnight and getting into his car and driving away.

'Such a delightful man,' declared her mother, collecting the coffee-cups. 'Supper's all ready. Do you suppose he enjoyed the mince pies?'

'Well, he ate almost all of them, so he must have done,' said Pamela. 'It's hard to think of him as a well-known man in his own particular field of medicine.'

Daisy turned to stare. 'Whatever makes you say that?' she asked.

'Well, he is, you know. I looked him up in the medical *Who's Who*. He's got a string of letters after his name and there's a whole lot about him.' She peeped at Daisy. 'Aren't you interested?'

'Not really,' said Daisy mendaciously.

Maisie was sitting up in bed looking better when Daisy went to see her during her lunchtime the next day, and there was no need to persuade her to do anything; the doctor had been to see her and everything was what she termed hunky-dory.

'Bless the pair of you,' declared Maisie, 'going to all that trouble; me and Milly and Whiskers are that grateful. Me own shower too and a bit of garden. I'm ter go 'ome in a week and just take things easy, like. 'Ow are yer getting on, ducks?'

'Just fine, Maisie. We've been promised part-time help for a day or two and the ward isn't busy.'

'Yer looking peaky. Working too 'ard, I'll be bound. P'raps you'll get a bit of an 'oliday when I get back.'

Daisy went back to the ward and started on the endless chores, glad of something to occupy her thoughts. At the end of the day when she went to tell Sister that she was ready to go, that young lady greeted her with the news that she and Philip were engaged. 'I'm going to tell everyone tomorrow morning, but I wanted you to know first, Daisy. Philip and I hope you'll come to our wedding.'

Daisy offered suitable congratulations, admired the diamond ring, hanging on a gold chain round Sister's neck under her uniform, and went off home. She was glad about Philip and Sister Carter; they would make a splendid pair. She must remember to write and congratulate him. It was to be hoped that someone as nice as Sister Carter would take over the ward; surely Dr Seymour would have a say in the matter?

She hadn't seen him that day and she guessed that he was back in London; indeed as she was leaving the hospital at the end of the day the hall porter handed her a letter addressed in an almost unreadable scrawl. It was from the doctor and very brief and to the point. Would she be so good as to go to Maisie's new home and make sure that everything was suitably arranged? It took a few minutes to decipher and it ended as abruptly as it had begun, with his initials.

'Written with the wrong end of a feather and with his eyes shut,' said Daisy to the empty hallway. All the same she tucked the missive safely away until she could put it under her pillow when she went to bed that night.

She could find no fault when she went to Maisie's new home that evening. It had been furnished with care, Maisie's bits and pieces polished, the bed made up. There was nothing for her to do but compliment her new landlady on the care which she had lavished upon her new lodger's room.

'Me and Mrs Trump,' she was told. 'Dr Seymour said as we were to make it as home-like as possible.' She beamed at Daisy. 'He's a real gentleman.'

Daisy had to work on Sunday for there was no one to relieve her but she was free on Saturday and she cycled to Lady Thorley's house in the afternoon. She had taken pains with her face and her hair, telling herself that since it was a birthday tea party it behoved her to make the best of her appearance. It was a pity that Lady Thorley had phoned in the morning to say that the car was being serviced and could she find her own way, but it was dry even if it was cold and she could wear her good shoes . . . And if at the back of her mind she was hoping that the doctor would be there she wasn't going to admit it.

He wasn't there. She was greeted rapturously by the twins, more soberly by Lady Thorley and their governess and informed that Sir Hugh wouldn't be home until evening. 'And Valentine, of course, is still in London— probably catching up on his social life.'

Despite her disappointment, Daisy enjoyed her afternoon; tea was a splendid meal and the birthday cake was magnificent and she had been led away to look at the presents, the best of which, Miss Thompson assured her, were a bead necklace threaded by Katie and a card-board box containing Josh's model of Belle in Plasticine. These needed to be admired at some length before Miss Thompson, asked what she would like to do since it was her birthday, diplomatically opted for a rousing game of snakes and ladders.

Daisy, promising to return in the not too distant future, went home a few hours later.

Salisbury was quiet when she went to work the next morning—a few people either going or coming from church, an infrequent car and several workers like herself. Even the hospital seemed quiet as she went up to the ward after changing into her pink pinny in the cloakroom used by the orderlies.

It wasn't quiet in the ward, of course. Most of the children were convalescing and making a fine racket, and since Sister had a weekend off and Staff Nurse was in charge they were noisier than usual; Staff Nurse was a splendid nurse but she lacked Sister's authority.

Daisy plunged into her day's routine, buoyed up by the news that there would be help in the morning. During her lunch break she went along to see Maisie and found her sitting by her bed, looking almost her old self.

'Can't wait ter get out of 'ere,' she confided to Daisy. 'The nurses are all right but that Sister—she's an old dragon. I wouldn't work 'ere for a fortune.'

'Well, you won't have to,' said Daisy. 'Sister can't wait to get you back.' She glanced at her watch. 'I must go— we all miss you, Maisie, really we do.'

Maisie looked pleased. 'Go on with you. Mrs Trump came ter see me yesterday—nice of 'er, weren't it? Thought I might like ter know about Milly and Whiskers. Very 'appy, she says.' She added wistfully, 'I'll be glad ter see them ...'

'They'll be glad to see you too, Maisie, and it won't be long now. You're all going to be so happy...'

The children were unruly that afternoon; mothers and fathers had come and they had become over-excited. They were allowed to visit any day they liked, of course, but the fathers were mostly at work and most of the mothers had other children or jobs, so Sunday afternoons saw an influx of mothers and fathers who stayed for the children's tea, so that they wouldn't eat, because they were excited or, worse, ate too much of the various biscuits and sweets which should have been handed over and very often weren't.

The last reluctant parent was ushered out finally and the nurses set about getting the children washed and ready for supper and bedtime, Daisy trotting to and fro with clean sheets, collecting up used bedlinen and bagging it, carrying mugs and plates out to the kitchen where an impatient maid, doing double duty since it was a Sunday, waited to wash up.

Stacking mugs and wiping down trays, Daisy became aware of a distant rumble. It wasn't thunder; it sounded like a vast crowd all talking at once but a long way off.

'Kids on the rampage,' said the maid crossly when Daisy mentioned it. And presently when the noise got nearer Staff Nurse made the same remark.

'A protest march or a rally, I dare say, marching through the town. Daisy, will you go down to the dispensary and get that Dettol Sister ordered? It didn't come up this morning and Night Nurse might need some during the night.' She picked up her pen to start the report. 'I've only got Nurse Stevens on and she's still feeding baby Price.'

Daisy made her way down two flights of stairs and along several corridors; most of the wards were at the back of the hospital and it was suppertime, early on Sundays. There was a pleasant smell of cooking as she nipped along, and her small nose twitched. As usual she had cut short her midday meal in order to have more time to spend with Maisie and now she was empty.

The dispenser on duty was on the point of going home and grumbled a good deal as he handed over the bottle. 'I don't know what this place is coming to,' he observed to no one in particular so that Daisy felt it unnecessary to answer him. She bade him goodnight and started on her way back.

It would be quicker if she used the main staircase from the entrance hall—strictly forbidden but there was no one around and it would save quite a few corridors. She reached the entrance hall, aware that the noise of a lot of people was growing louder by the minute; they sounded rather out of hand too. It was to be hoped that they would go past the hospital quickly.

She had her foot on the bottom stair when she realised that they weren't going past; the shouts and yells were very close now—they must be in the forecourt. Even as she thought it the double doors were flung open and a dozen or more youths came through them. They were laughing and shouting and ripe for mischief and she looked towards the porter's lodge. There was always someone on duty there; they could telephone for help—get the police...

It was apparent to her after a moment that there wasn't anyone there. The corridors on either side of her were empty, the rooms which led out of them would be empty too—the consultant's room, Matron's office, the hospital secretary's, and on the other side the committee room which took up almost all of one side of the corridor.

The youths had hesitated at the sight of her but now they were dribbling in, two and three at a time. Some of them had what looked to her like clubs and one of them, bolder than the others, was chipping the bust of a long-dead consultant of the hospital; he was the first in a row and Daisy felt sick at the idea of the damage he could cause. He had a knife; she shook with fright—she was terrified of knives. Her mouth had gone dry too and she clasped her hands in front of her to stop them trembling; all the same she stayed where she was.

'Go away at once,' she called in a voice which wobbled alarmingly; 'this is a hospital...'

The hooligans hooted with raucous laughter. 'An' you're the matron?' yelled someone. 'Try and stop us...' Those behind surged forward and the leaders came nearer, taking a swipe at a second bust, this time of the hospital's founder, as they did so.

Daisy had put the Dettol bottle down when she had turned to see what the commotion was; now she picked it up and held it clasped in both hands in front of her. It wasn't exactly a weapon but if she threw it ... First she tried again; rage had swallowed at least part of her fear. 'Get out,' she bawled, 'you louts. The police will be here any moment now.'

This was greeted by jeers and bad language, a good deal of which she didn't understand, which was a good thing, although she had an idea that it was unprintable.

The lout who had been swiping at the marble busts edged nearer and her shaking hands tightened on the bottle ...

A great arm encircled her waist and lifted her gently, to push her with equal gentleness behind Dr Seymour's vast back.

'Just in time,' said the doctor placidly. 'I do believe you were going to waste a bottle of Dettol.'

Daisy got her breath back. 'Valentine,' she muttered before she had stopped to think, and heaven alone knew what she might have said next if he hadn't said in a quite ordinary voice,

'Get help, my darling, and ring the police, just in case they don't already know ...'

'They'll kill you,' said Daisy into the fine cloth of his jacket. 'I'm not going to leave you ...'

'Do as I say, Daisy, run along.'

There was no gainsaying that voice; she turned and flew up the staircase and tore along the corridor until she reached the men's medical ward.

The charge nurse at the other end of the long ward looked up as she raced down its length.

'Mr Soames—there's a mob of hooligans in the hall; Dr Seymour's there, he needs help, and I'm to ring the police.'

Mr Soames was already walking up the ward, beckoning two male nurses to follow as he went. 'Ring the police then the porter's room and the housemen's flat. The numbers are by the phone on my desk.' He paused for a moment by a student nurse. 'You're in charge until we get back.'

He opened the ward doors and Daisy heard Dr Seymour's voice quite clearly. It wasn't particularly loud but it sounded authoritative and very calm. She went into Mr Soames' office and dialled 999. The police were already on their way, she was told; she hung up and dialled the porters' room and then the housemen's flat and a few minutes later heard feet thundering down the staircase. She still had the bottle of Dettol with her; she picked it up and carried it carefully up another flight of stairs to the children's ward and gave it to Staff Nurse.

'There's a frightful racket going on,' said that young lady, 'and you've been ages, Daisy.'

'Some hooligans broke into the hospital, Staff.' For the life of her she couldn't say any more, only stared at the other girl from a white face.

'A cup of tea,' said Staff. 'Sit yourself down. Did you get caught up in it?' When she nodded Staff added, 'A good thing it's time for you to go off duty.' She fetched the tea. 'Sit there for a bit—it must have been upsetting.' She eyed Daisy's ashen face and decided that she would have to wait to find out what was happening. There was a good deal of noise now, loud men's voices and heavy feet tramping around, luckily not so close as to disturb the children.

Daisy drank her tea. Everything had happened rather fast and she was terribly bewildered, but one thing she remembered with clarity. She had called the doctor Valentine and he had called her his darling. 'Get help, my darling,' he had said, but perhaps he had said that just to make her listen...

The phone rang and she supposed she had better answer it.

'Stay where you are until I come for you,' said the doctor in her ear. 'In the children's ward?'

'Yes.' She suddenly wanted to cry.

The phone went dead and she sat down again and presently Staff Nurse came back to write the report.

'Feeling better?' she asked kindly. 'Dr Cowie was in the ward just now; he said they'd cleared those louts away. You were very brave, Daisy, standing there all alone, telling them to go away. Weren't you scared?'

'I've never been so frightened in my life before; I think I would have run away if Dr Seymour hadn't come.'

'He said you were magnificent.' Staff glanced at Daisy's face. 'If it had been me I'd have cut and run.'

'I was too frightened,' said Daisy. 'I don't suppose I could have moved.' She smiled at the other girl, who reflected that Sister had been right—Daisy wasn't the usual sort of orderly; she wondered why she had taken the job...

The door opened and Dr Seymour walked in unhurriedly. 'Get your coat,' he told Daisy, 'I'll take you home. Feel all right now?'

Daisy frowned; he had made it sound as though she had had the screaming hysterics. 'I'm perfectly all right, thank you, Doctor.'

'Good. I'll be in the entrance hall in five minutes.' He held the door open for her and she bade Staff Nurse goodnight and went past him, her chin lifted.

In the car she asked presently, 'What happened to all those hooligans?'

'The police carted some of them off, the rest ran away. Very few of them were locals.'

His voice was casual; he couldn't have been more impersonal. She felt too discouraged to say anything else. As he stopped outside her home she made haste to get out, to be stopped by his hand on the door. 'Not so fast. I'm coming in.'

'There's no need,' she assured him but that was a waste of breath; he got out, opened her door and urged her through the gate as the door opened.

Before she could say a word her mother said, 'Oh, my dear—are you all right? What a dreadful thing to have happened—were you very frightened? And how can I ever thank you, Dr Seymour, for rescuing her as you did?'

'Hardly a rescue, Mrs Pelham.' He had pushed Daisy gently ahead of him so that they were all standing in the little hall. 'I happened to be passing—I'm sure Daisy would have coped very well on her own.'

'Well, of course, she's a very sensible girl,' agreed her mother. Nevertheless, I do thank you.' She hesitated. 'I dare say you're a busy man, but if you would like a cup of coffee . . . ?'

'That would be delightful.'

Daisy hadn't said a word; he still had a hand on her shoulder, and now he turned her round, unbuttoned her coat and took it off, pulled the gloves from her hands and propelled her briskly into the kitchen where he sat her down in a chair, took a chair himself and fell into cheerful conversation with Pamela. It wasn't until Mrs Pelham had handed round the coffee and offered cake that Pamela asked, 'Were you scared, Daisy?'

Daisy put her cup down carefully, burst into tears and darted out of the room. Mrs Pelham looked alarmed, Pamela surprised and the doctor undisturbed.

'No, Mrs Pelham, leave her alone for a while. She'll be all right but she had a nasty shock and the reaction has set in. She was remarkably brave—you would have been very proud of her. Tomorrow she'll be quite herself again; bed is the best place for her now and perhaps a warm drink before she sleeps.' He added kindly, 'You mustn't worry.'

Mrs Pelham said faintly, 'She's such a dear girl...'

'Indeed she is,' agreed the doctor, and something in his voice made Pamela stare at him.

'Are you in love with her?' she asked, and ignored her mother's shocked indrawn breath.

'Oh, yes,' said the doctor blandly and smiled at Pamela. 'I must go. The coffee was delicious, Mrs Pelham.' He said his goodbyes and Pamela went to the door with him.

'I won't tell,' she told him. He smiled then and dropped a kiss on her cheek before he went away.

He had been quite right, of course; Daisy slept like a baby all night, ate her breakfast and cycled to work, quite restored to her normal sensible self. She felt ashamed of her outburst in front of the doctor and as soon as she saw him she would apologise. It was a great pity that she had called him Valentine to his face like that, but he would surely realise that she had been upset at the time. She rehearsed a neat little speech as she cycled and presented herself in the ward nicely primed.

It wasn't until the end of the day that Sister mentioned in Daisy's hearing that he had gone to Holland. 'Lectures or something,' she explained to Staff Nurse. 'He does get around, doesn't he? I should have loved to see him telling those louts where they could go...'

Daisy, collecting the sheets and listening with both ears, wondered forlornly if she would see him again.

Sooner than she expected. It was two days later as she was collecting the children's mugs after their morning milk that one of the nurses told her that she was wanted in Sister's office. Daisy put down her tray, twitched her pink pinny into neatness and knocked on the office door, and when there was no answer poked her head round it. Her eyes met Dr Seymour's steady gaze and since she could hardly withdraw without saying something she said, 'Oh, I'm sorry, sir, I was told to come here but Sister isn't...' She tailed off, not sure what to say next, anxious to be gone even though her heart was beating a tattoo at the sight of him.

'No, she isn't,' agreed the doctor calmly. 'Come in, Daisy.'

He got up from the chair behind the desk, closed the door behind her. 'Do sit down,' he said and when she shook her head came to stand so close to her that all she could see was an expanse of dark grey superfine wool waistcoat. She counted the buttons and lifted her gaze sufficiently to study his tie—a very fine one, silk and vaguely striped. Italian, no doubt. Higher than that she refused to look while she strove to remember the speech she had rehearsed so carefully.

'I had no idea,' said the doctor at last, 'that courting a young lady could be fraught with so many difficulties. Why is it, I wonder, that I'm able to diagnose acute anterior poliomyelitis, measles, hydrocephalus, intersusception, inflamed adenoids, the common cold…and yet I find myself unable to find the right words?'

He was smiling down at her and she said with a little gasp, 'Oh, do be careful what you're saying; you might regret it—I dare say you're very tired or something.' She added urgently, 'I'm the orderly…'

His laughter rumbled. 'Oh, no, you're not, you're Daisy, my Daisy, the most darling girl in the world and so hard to pin down. I'm in love with you, my darling, have been since the first moment I set eyes on you…'

She looked up into his face then. 'But you never…' she began.

'You'd made up your mind that we didn't like each other, hadn't you? You are, my dearest heart, pigheaded at times.' He made that sound like a compliment. 'It seemed that I needed to be circumspect.' He wrapped great arms around her. 'You called me Valentine,' he reminded her, 'and you wanted to stay with me. You looked at me with those lovely grey eyes and I knew then that whatever you said it would make no difference, that you loved me too.'

'But I'm an…' began Daisy, and then added, 'Yes, I do love you.'

She didn't finish because he kissed her then. Presently he said, 'You'll marry me, my little love? And soon.'

She lifted her face from his shoulder. 'I have to give a week's notice.'

'Rubbish. I'll deal with that at once.'

'But you can't...'

'Oh, yes, I can and I will. You'll leave this evening.' He kissed her gently, 'My love, leave everything to me.'

She smiled mistily. 'I must go, Valentine—the milk-mugs...'

He kissed her once more and opened the door for her. 'I can't believe it's true,' she told him. 'What will everyone say?'

He caught her hand and held it for a moment. 'We'll ask them at our wedding. I'll be waiting outside for you this evening, my darling.' He smiled. 'The end of my waiting.'

Daisy nodded, her head full of glimpses of a delightful future. She stood on tiptoe and kissed his cheek and whisked herself away, back to her tray of mugs. But not for long.

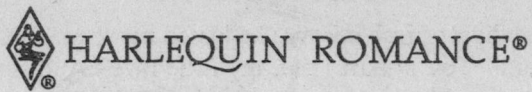 # HARLEQUIN ROMANCE®

brings you

More Romances Celebrating Love, Families and Children!

Next month, look out for Emma Goldrick's new book,
Leonie's Luck, Harlequin Romance #3351
(a heart-warming story of romantic involvement between
Leonie Marshal and Charlie Wheeler, who marches
without warning—or permission—into her life!)

Charlie's nine-year-old daughter, Cecilia, who comes to
live with them—at Leonie's Aunt Agnes's invitation—is
somehow never far from what is going on and plays an
innocent part in bringing them together!

Available wherever Harlequin books are sold.

Fifty red-blooded, white-hot, true-blue hunks
from every State in the Union!

Look for MEN MADE IN AMERICA! Written by some
of our most popular authors, these stories feature some
of the strongest, sexiest men, each from a different state
in the union!

Two titles available every month at your favorite
retail outlet.

In February, look for:

THE SECURITY MAN by Dixie Browning
(North Carolina)
A CLASS ACT by Kathleen Eagle (North Dakota)

In March, look for:

TOO NEAR THE FIRE by Lindsay McKenna (Ohio)
A TIME AND A SEASON by Curtiss Ann Matlock
(Oklahoma)

You won't be able to resist MEN MADE IN AMERICA!

If you are looking for more titles by

BETTY NEELS

Don't miss this chance to order additional stories by one of Harlequin's best-loved authors:

Harlequin Romance®

#03249	ROMANTIC ENCOUNTER	$2.89	☐
#03267	A HAPPY MEETING	$2.99	☐
#03279	THE QUIET PROFESSOR	$2.99	☐
#03299	TWO FOR THE HEART*	$2.99	☐
#03315	A GIRL IN A MILLION	$2.99 U.S.	☐
		$3.50 CAN.	☐
#03323	AT ODDS WITH LOVE	$2.99 U.S.	☐
		$3.50 CAN.	☐
#03339	THE AWAKENED HEART	$2.99 U.S.	☐
		$3.50 CAN.	☐

*a short story collection with Ellen James
(limited quantities available on certain titles)

TOTAL AMOUNT	$
POSTAGE & HANDLING	$
($1.00 for one book, 50¢ for each additional)	
APPLICABLE TAXES*	$ _____
TOTAL PAYABLE	$ _____
(check or money order—please do not send cash)	

To order, complete this form and send it, along with a check or money order for the total above, payable to Harlequin Books, to: **In the U.S.:** 3010 Walden Avenue, P.O. Box 9047, Buffalo, NY 14269-9047; **In Canada:** P.O. Box 613, Fort Erie, Ontario, L2A 5X3.

Name: _____

Address: _____ City: _____

State/Prov.: _____ Zip/Postal Code: _____

*New York residents remit applicable sales taxes.   HBNBACK3

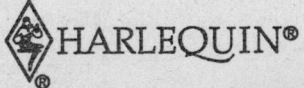

HARLEQUIN®